THE
PRODIGAL

SUSANNE O'LEARY

Cover design and typesetting by J.D. Smith Design

Edited by Julie Freed, Free Range Editorial

CHAPTER 1

Dessie had only worked at Smythe's Auctioneers in Mayfair for a week when she got the assignment. The envelope was addressed to "Miss Desdemona Broadbent," and she thought at first it was an invitation to a party. But all she found was a scribbled note in spidery handwriting that said: *Please see me regarding sale of contents of country house. Best, Martin Smythe.*

Martin Smythe. The managing director. He wanted to see her about this house, wherever it was. She read the note again. He didn't say when she was to see him, or where. Probably in his office; that inner sanctum she had never been allowed to enter, being a lowly apprentice only just arrived at the small but reputable auction house. There was only one way to find out about this assignment.

Dessie got up from her desk at the back of the communal office, straightened her skirt, tucked her white shirt into the waistband, and smoothed her hair. It was coming up to five o'clock, and she hoped Mr Smythe was still in his office.

He was. "Come in," he boomed when she knocked softly on the massive mahogany door.

She pushed the door open to discover the broad back of the managing director, who was standing in the middle of the oriental carpet tapping golf balls into a silver bowl.

"Hello, Mr Smythe," she said. "I'm Dessie Broadbent. You sent me a—"

"Don't move. Don't even breathe. I have to get…" He tapped the club gently on the last ball, and it rolled slowly into the bowl, making a click as it hit the side. "Bingo." Smythe turned around and beamed. "See that? A perfect putt."

Dessie nodded. "Congratulations."

"You play golf?"

"No."

"Oh. Right." He straightened up, walked across the floor to a huge desk littered with papers and catalogues, and sat down in a leather armchair that had seen better days. "Desdemona…"

"Broadbent," she filled in. "But everyone calls me Dessie. You sent me a note."

"Oh, yes…" He riffled through the papers. "About the house… Sit down. I have the details here…"

Dessie sat down on the edge of a lyre back chair. Regency, she noted, possibly very early nineteenth century. She folded her hands in her lap and put her feet neatly together, waiting for Smythe to speak. He was a big man in his sixties with a ruddy complexion, small pale blue eyes, and thinning white hair. Managing director of the auction house, which was not quite Sotheby's or Christie's but reputable and old all the same. They were famous for the gems they had unearthed in what they called "Sleeping Beauty" auctions of houses that had been deserted for decades but never sold, their contents often treasure troves of art and silverware. Dessie itched to know what this one would be. She waited patiently while Martin Smythe looked through his papers, muttering under his breath.

He looked up, waving a piece of paper. "Here it is. Sorry to keep you waiting. It's an Irish property. In—" he peered at the note "—County Tipperary. A property called Killybeg House. Near a town called Cloughmichael."

Dessie's mouth was suddenly dry, and her heart nearly stopped. *No. Not Killybeg. Please let that be a mistake.*

Smythe peered at her over his glasses. "You're from Ireland, is that correct?"

"Yes. But I left," she said. "A long time ago." As if that would make her less Irish.

"But still," Martin Smythe said, "Irish. Knowing about the country and antiques of that area, no?"

Dessie nodded. "I suppose." He was right. She did have extensive knowledge of the antique furniture one might find in an Irish country house. She had worked briefly at an auction house in Dublin and had become fascinated by the history of country houses in Ireland, making it her speciality. It was on her CV too, she remembered.

"Good." He kept looking at her. "You have the most extraordinary eyes." He leaned forward. "I can't quite see what colour…"

Dessie met his gaze without blinking. She was used to this. "Dark green," she replied.

"Ah, yes." He sat back. "Please forgive me. Didn't mean to get personal. It was just that your colouring is so—unusual. Those dark, greenish eyes with that black hair and pale skin… so very Irish. And the accent, of course."

"Well, sure I'm Oirish," Dessie quipped with a stiff smile.

"Very much so, I hear," Smythe replied without raising an eyebrow. He nodded, resuming his businesslike air. "Right then, let's give you the details. This house is quite a find. It hasn't been lived in for over seventy years. But a housekeeper has been on the premises and has been keeping an eye on the place, making sure it was aired and dusted and even heated in the winter according to the wishes of the owners. But now the owners—or owner, I should say, as there is only one left, has…"

She looked up. "Died?" she whispered, her heart constricting. It couldn't be…Richard was only a few years older than her. He couldn't—

"No," Martin Smythe said. "Maybe I should explain the

circumstances. The house is owned by the descendant of a man who worked as an engineer for the British Empire. He left at the beginning of the twentieth century and returned thirty years later, when his parents died. Incredible to think of all that happened during his long absence. The First World War, the Irish War of Independence... A Rip Van Winkle kind of story, I imagine. In any case, this man—Tom Hourigan— was married with two children, but the family moved to America after the wife died in the early 1940s. It hasn't been lived in since, as the family settled in the US. And now the children of Tom Hourigan have passed away, and their only heir has decided to sell the contents; the house will be up for sale later. I believe he's getting married and has no wish to live in the house." Martin Smythe drew breath.

Dessie felt the colour drain from her face as another shock wave hit her. Richard getting married again? It couldn't be true. Why couldn't he have died instead? "I see," she mumbled.

"So, we'll be doing the cataloguing first," Smythe continued. "It's a big house with a lot of artefacts and such, we've been told. But we have no actual details, except for some of the paintings, which are surprisingly valuable for a house in such a God-forgotten place." He let out a small grunt. "The Irish were sly when it came to hiding their wealth. In those days, I mean," he added after a quick look at Dessie over his glasses. "You look a little pale, m'dear. Not feeling quite the thing?"

Dessie cleared her dry throat. "Just a cold, that's all. I'm fine, really."

He nodded. "Good, good. Then you'll have recovered by the time you go to Ireland. I thought you'd be perfect for this job, as you have an inside knowledge of the country and seem to have a knack for assessing artefacts and such, especially of things Irish. Am I right?"

Dessie nodded. "Yes. I have a degree in art history, and

my thesis touched on the subject of art and antiques in Ireland." She paused. "But…I'm not sure I can tackle such a big assignment on my own. I mean cataloguing such a house…"

Smythe let out a jovial laugh. "You won't be on your own. I see this as part of your training. One of our directors will be coming with you to supervise and do a lot of the cataloguing too."

"I see. Which one of the directors?" Dessie asked, praying it wouldn't be Amanda Jones, a snooty bitch with bad breath.

"My son, Marcus. You've met him?"

"Yes. Once." She remembered a good-looking, suave, and slightly distant man. He hadn't done more than nod in her direction when they were introduced a few weeks earlier. Then he had disappeared to Scotland to conduct an auction. She hadn't seen him since.

"Excellent," Smythe breezed on, pulling a piece of paper from a pile on the desk. "Here are all the details. Accommodation has been arranged as well. You'll be staying in the gatehouse with the housekeeper, who has offered two of the rooms and use of the kitchen for you both. The auction is scheduled to take place in late December, so you have two months to complete the job, and then we can print the catalogue. I suggest you get to Ireland as soon as you can to start sorting out the contents of the house. Marcus is flying to Dublin tonight. I hope you can be ready to go in a couple of days. My secretary will book your ticket."

Dessie looked at him while she thought. There was no way out, no plausible excuse. It was a fabulous assignment, a great opportunity to show off her skills. This auction would make headlines across Ireland and in other countries too. Any apprentice would be delighted to get this chance to shine. A shortcut to a permanent position. "Thank you," she said and got up, rubbing her clammy palms against her skirt. "I'll let her know when I'm ready to go."

"Good." Smythe picked up a folder. "Here are some notes and a brief history of the house. We need more information so we can include it in the catalogue. When the house was built, the original owners, and so on. Maybe you could do some research on all of that?"

Dessie took the folder. "No problem."

"A lot of work. Hope you don't mind."

"Of course not. It won't be that hard," Dessie replied, knowing it was true. She wouldn't have to do much research on the house and its history. She knew all about it already.

* * *

Dessie was on the point of pulling out of the trip numerous times during the following days. But that could mean having to give up a job and a career that had been her dream for the past few years. In order to pay her college fees, she'd worked two jobs while she finished her degree at Trinity College in Dublin. The dream had kept her going while she stretched the pennies as far as they would go—living cheaply, eating badly, and squeezing in as much fun as she could manage between jobs and exams. And here she was in London, working at this classy establishment and getting a great assignment in one of those high-profile auctions. A fantastic opportunity—if only it weren't *that* house.

Cloughmichael—her home town, where her heart had broken, never to mend. Going back would be laced with pain and shame. How could she face people there again? How could she go back to her family and see the loathing in their eyes? It didn't seem possible. Dessie struggled with the problem as she packed and prepared to leave the small flat in Battersea she shared with two other girls—both career women working in the City. They wouldn't miss her while she was gone. They could even sublet her room to someone who was more like them—upper class and coolly sophisticated.

Dessie put clothes suitable for the Irish countryside in November on her bed, feeling very much like a lamb going to slaughter. She stacked jeans, cardigans, shirts, thermal vests, and warm socks in a wobbly pile as her heart sank. There was no way out. She had to go if she wanted to hang on to her job. She pulled a green wool sweater from a drawer and held it up against her in front of the mirror. Green, like Ireland, like the rolling hills and fields. How hard—but oh, how sweet—to come home after all the years away. She hugged the sweater and closed her eyes. Maybe it was meant to be? Maybe this would give her closure and peace? She nodded to herself and put the sweater on the pile. Yes. It was right. It was time. Time to go home.

CHAPTER 2

Dublin Airport was quiet, with only a straggly line at passport control. Dessie showed her passport, went through the gate, and walked down the long corridor to the baggage area. How strange it was to be back. The airport looked like any airport in any part of the world, but there was still that unmistakable Irish feel to it. Was it the advertisements for Guinness and trips to the Cliffs of Moher and other points of scenic beauty? Or the sound of Irish voices here and there? Or Irish laughter and shouts of "Where's the craic?" that made her feel instantly at home? Whatever it was, it gave her a dart of joy and excitement mixed with fear. How would *they* react to her returning after all that had happened? But whatever they said or did, she was home at last. *I'll deal with it*, she thought as she pulled her heavy suitcase from the conveyor belt. *It'll be hard, but it'll be all right in the end.* That inner voice didn't quite convince her. But she had to look as if she believed it. Her back straight, her head held high, she walked through customs and out through the exit into the arrivals area.

Dessie felt a pang of sadness that there was nobody to meet her but then marched on, dragging her suitcase, telling herself to get a grip. She had a long trip ahead: first, the bus to Heuston Station, then the train and, finally, the country bus that reeked of wet wool and dogs, until she arrived at the bus depot in Cloughmichael.

A tap on her shoulder made her jump. A voice she didn't recognise said: "Desdemona?"

She turned around and looked up at a tall man with curly light brown hair, dressed in a battered Burberry trench coat and a baseball cap with the logo of the Oxford rowing team. There were crinkles around his blue eyes and a dimple appeared at the corner of his mouth as he smiled at her.

He pulled off his cap. "Hello," he said. "I'm—"

"Marcus Smythe," she interrupted. "We met a couple of weeks ago."

He put his cap back on his head. "That's right. We did. Otherwise, I wouldn't have known you."

Dessie let out a thin little laugh. "Of course not. Sorry. That was stupid."

"Not at all. Relax. I'm not going to eat you. Let me take your bag."

"Er…okay…" She let go of the suitcase and let him drag it along. "But what—"

"What am I doing here?" He stopped walking, nearly making her trip. "I drove over here in my car. Came on that dreadful ferry a couple of days ago. Thought I'd pick you up when I heard you were arriving today. Just to get to know each other and all that."

"Oh. I see."

He glanced at her. "You don't sound terribly pleased."

"Oh, I am. I was just surprised to see you. Sorry," she said again.

"No need to apologise." He started walking again. "I found a parking space quite close to the entrance. Follow me."

They didn't talk during the short walk across the street, the quick pause at the ticket machine, or the long trundle down the concrete path to his car—a dark blue Alfa Romeo.

Marcus pressed the key, and the lights blinked for a second, emitting a noise between a squeak and a ping. He opened the boot and put Dessie's suitcase beside an assortment of luggage and plastic bags.

"You've a lot of stuff," Dessie couldn't help remarking.

"I did a little shopping while I was in Dublin. Stocked up on wine and got a few items of clothing, as I was short of hiking gear and riding boots."

Dessie nodded. "Good idea."

"There's good hunting in Tipperary, I've heard. Do you ride?"

"I used to. But I haven't been on a horse in years."

"I'm sure it'd all come back to you."

"I don't intend to find out." Dessie opened the passenger door. "Let's get going, then, or we'll get stuck in the evening traffic."

"Yes, your ladyship," Marcus quipped and got in beside her. He started the car and expertly backed out of the space.

Dessie sank back against the soft leather and wished she were miles away, on that rickety train instead of in this smooth car with someone who made her feel awkward and stupid. She glanced at him as he put the ticket into the slot at the exit. He had a nice voice with that unmistakeable cut-glass accent of the upper classes. Eton, Oxford, rowing club, fox hunting, Pimm's at Ascot—it was all there, in his voice. *Bloody toff,* she thought and met his gaze with a cold glare.

"Anything wrong?" he asked. "I've a spot on my chin? Or spinach between my teeth? Please tell me, so I can fix it."

She looked away, her face hot. "No, there's nothing wrong at all. It's me."

"It's you?" He was forced to keep his eyes on the road as they came to the intersection. "What's the matter?" he asked as they reached the connecting road to the M50.

"Nothing." She slid down in the seat. "I'm just tired. Jet lag or something."

He laughed and glanced at her. "Jet lag? After a forty-five-minute flight?"

"Yeah, well, whatever. Just ignore me, okay?" Dessie slid further down in the seat and turned her head to look out the window, instantly regretting her outburst. He probably had her taped as a complete weirdo by now. But she didn't care. His opinion of her was the least of her worries. How she was going to handle her return to Cloughmichael was at the top of her list of problems.

She was jolted out of her thoughts as the car came to a screeching halt on the hard shoulder of the motorway. She turned her head and met Marcus' blazing eyes.

He hit the steering wheel with his palm. "What the *fuck* is wrong with you? I haven't said more than a polite hello, and you're acting like a martyr. If you don't explain what's going on in that pretty little head of yours, I'll have to ask you to get out."

Dessie sat up. "Get out? Here? Where will I go?"

"I don't give a shit," Marcus snarled. "I'm not spending the next two hours with some angry little bitch with no manners. Get your act together or you'll lose both this ride and your job."

"Is this a threat?" Dessie snarled.

"No, sweetheart," Marcus purred, "it's a bloody promise."

They glared at each other.

Dessie swallowed a sob and fumbled with the door handle. Then she gave up. He had her up against the wall. She slumped against the seat and closed her eyes. "Okay. You win." She opened her eyes and looked at him. "I'm struggling with something big, something...well, quite unbearable, if you must know."

He nodded, his eyes cold. "Yes, I must. Go on."

"Don't look at me while I tell you," she ordered.

"All right." He stared through the windscreen. "Tell me, then, and make it quick. The traffic's getting worse."

She plucked at a thread on the sleeve of her green sweater. "It's like this," she started. "I was born in Cloughmichael and grew up there. I left ten years ago after…something I did caused a huge scandal."

"I see. What did you do? Kiss the parish priest?"

"Much worse. And it's not funny. Nor will I tell you what it was."

He nodded. "Fair enough. I won't ask. So, this is why you're so uptight?"

"Yes."

"And you're all tense about showing your face there again? In fact, you're terrified. But you couldn't refuse this assignment because you don't want to lose the job?"

"Yes," she said again. "That's the gist of it."

He nodded and turned to look at her. "It's okay. I understand," he said, his voice softer. "You have nothing to fear from me. If you want to bail out now, I'll drive you back to Dublin. Then you can get a flight back to London. I'll make up something to tell my father. You won't lose your job."

She looked at him for a moment while she considered his offer. A way out. It was tempting. She was on the verge of accepting when something made her change her mind. A thought, a sudden feeling. It was as if she had reached a crossroads with a signpost pointing at a road full of obstacles. And even though she couldn't see what was at the end, she knew it was the way to go. She shook her head. "No thanks. I have to go back home and face—"

"Face what?" he asked, sounding amused. "The music?"

"*Them*," she mumbled. "I can't go forward if I don't go back. Sounds daft, doesn't it?"

"No. I know what you mean. And I think you're frightfully brave." He started the car. "Let's get going, then. You can fill me in on this town we're going to while we drive. I assume you know all about Killybeg House too."

"Yes, I do. I didn't have to do any research on it," she added with a smile.

He laughed. "Of course you didn't. You feel like telling me about it? The history and such, I mean."

"Of course. I know it all by heart."

"Perfect. Let's hear it, then. It'll entertain me while I drive."

Dessie sat up, folded her hands in her lap, and began to tell Marcus Smythe the story of the house.

"Killybeg was created a baronetcy in the eighteenth century for a British nobleman who was knighted by King George for some bravery or other in some war or other." Dessie laughed apologetically. "Sorry. Not very into British aristocracy, I'm afraid."

"Minor aristocracy in any case," Marcus quipped. "Probably someone in trade who did something for the Prince Regent and was then given property in Ireland. But do go on."

"Yes, well…The house was built for him—the nobleman, I mean, not the Prince Regent—in 1801."

"So, a Georgian house, then," Marcus commented. "No earlier house on the site?"

"There was an old castle there once. I think Killybeg was built on the foundations. It's a lovely house with two stories over basement—"

"I know. I've seen photos. Marvellous architecture. And inside, I think the best part is that huge cantilevered staircase. A graceful spiral that goes up into the top floor."

"And the windows. All the original sash windows are still there."

"I know. But tell me more about the people who lived there. This English nobleman, did he own the house for long?"

"No. He had to sell it to pay his gambling debts. It was bought in 1820 by an Irishman called O'Connor who had made a fortune in the retail business, making cloth and uniforms for the British navy fighting in the Napoleonic Wars. Clever man, who made the cloth from his own sheep grazing on his land. An Irish Catholic too, which is amazing, if you know Irish history. His brother became what he called 'a red-hot Protestant.' But the Catholic branch of the family prospered because they were distantly related to Lord Lismore. Another Irish lord."

"Aha," Marcus said, his eyes on the road ahead, winding through green fields and meadows. "Fascinating. So they were responsible for the earlier pieces in the house?"

"Yes. The George IV and William IV furniture in the house is probably from the O'Connor period," Dessie said. "And the oriental pieces must have come from the Hourigan family, who bought the house in the late nineteenth century. Two of the sons worked in India and China in the service of the British Commonwealth."

"Oh, yes. And one of them came back after thirty years away and then married a foreign woman. I believe the family lived there until the 1940s and then it was locked up until now. Nobody has lived there for nearly seventy years."

"Yes, something like that. Except one family member came back for a visit during the summer once. I believe," Dessie added, trying to keep the tremor out of her voice. Oh God, that summer…when Richard Hourigan had arrived from America to inspect Killybeg. That summer, when she had just turned nineteen, and her life had changed forever.

Marcus' voice cut into Dessie's thoughts. "I'd like to stop for tea. I feel a little peckish. How about you?"

Dessie glanced at the clock on the dashboard. It was nearly five o'clock. She was quite hungry, having had very little to eat since lunchtime. "Sounds good. I think there's some place in Kildare that does—"

"How about there?" Marcus pointed at a sign. "Junction fourteen, petrol station with restaurant. Won't that do?"

"Never heard of it. But then, I haven't been in this country for ten years. This part of the motorway wasn't even built then."

Marcus drove into the exit. "Probably fine. I'm sure they

do tea and buns. It'll tide us over until supper time. I believe the housekeeper in the gate lodge has promised to feed us tonight."

"The housekeeper?" Dessie realised that she hadn't even thought about this woman. Who was she? The gate lodge hadn't been lived in for years when she left. The house had been looked after by the wife of a local farmer in those days.

"Her name is Audrey. She's also the editor of the local newspaper. That's all I know. Some elderly journalist who gets free lodgings in return for a bit of housework, is my guess."

"Don't think I know her." Dessie relaxed. Not anyone from the old days. "I have a feeling the gate lodge will be a little primitive," she added. "Nice house, but as far as I know, not what you might be used to."

"You mean no central heating, limited hot water, and a Victorian bathroom?"

"Something like that."

"Sounds just like boarding school." Marcus pulled into the parking lot beside the petrol station and looked out at the state-of-the-art building beside it with a neon sign that said "Hot food served all day." "Well, ma'am, afternoon tea for two, eh?"

Dessie laughed. "Burger and fries more likely. But I'm sure they can give us a cup of tea. I need a pit stop anyway."

Marcus winked. "Let's enjoy the facilities while we can. The gate lodge might turn out to be quite a challenge. But perhaps it will be interesting to step back in time?"

Dessie sighed. "I love history, but I'm not sure I want to experience it personally."

"It might put manners on us," Marcus said. "We're all getting terribly spoilt." He went around the car and opened the door for Dessie. "After you, princess."

Startled, Dessie looked back at him. Was he making fun of her? But his bland expression gave her no clues about his feelings—if any. He'd be a tough nut to crack.

* * *

As darkness fell, Dessie was struck by how very black the nights were in the country. No streetlights illuminated the road, no flashing neon signs, bright shopfronts or lights from windows. Here, the curtains of the houses they passed were drawn against the cold, wet evening, and the smell of turf fires mingled with a whiff of damp earth and dead leaves. It was dark by the time they reached the outskirts of Cloughmichael. As they drove into town and down the main street, she noticed how much the town had changed since she left. Where once there had been small shops and businesses, there were now only empty shopfronts. Where were the hairdressers, the butchers, the shoe shop and the news agency? Why did the town look so desolate and forlorn?

"What happened?" she said, bewildered.

"How do you mean?" Marcus asked.

"This street used to be full of little shops. The only things left are the pub and the bookmakers."

Marcus shrugged. "Progress, I suppose. Big supermarkets taking over. Shopping centres on the outskirts of towns and villages. I've seen it happen in England too. Pity."

"Yes." Dessie felt tears welling up, and there was a hard knot in her stomach as they turned the corner and drove past the church and the old building beside it.

"Nice church," Marcus said.

"Yes. Protestant. Built by Nash. Early 1800s."

"And that lovely Georgian building beside it? The vicarage?"

Dessie closed her eyes. "Yes," she whispered.

Marcus glanced at her through the gloom. "Brings back memories?"

Dessie nodded, clasping her hands in her lap. "I grew up there. My dad was the vicar."

"You're the daughter of a vicar?" Marcus' voice was incredulous. "I'd never have guessed."

She sat up and stared at him. "Why not? Is there a vicar's daughter look? And in that case what would it be? Pleated skirts, pearls, cardigans, and sensible shoes?"

He laughed out loud. "No, not quite. But your accent… pure Irish without a hint of British refinement."

"I went to a local school. My parents wanted me to grow up like any Irish girl."

He nodded. "Commendable, I have to say. But it's not just that brogue. You don't have the demure look one would expect. I have a feeling you're quite feisty at times."

Dessie shot him a cheeky smile. "Feisty? If that's what you want to call it. I can go from sweetheart to bitch in two seconds flat if I'm cornered."

"Thanks for the warning. I'll try not to corner you."

"Good idea."

They were silent as the car swept out of town and on through the dark landscape. Marcus stopped once to consult the map on his phone at a crossroads. "Left here, I think," he muttered.

"Yes. Left, then right and down a boreen until you reach the gate," Dessie cut in.

Marcus put away his phone. "Boreen?"

"Country lane in Irish English."

"I keep forgetting you're a native." He put the car in first gear and took a sharp left, then a right down a tiny road with a strip of grass in the middle. "A road not much travelled, I see."

"It never was, except in the glory days of the British Empire."

"You sound surprisingly Republican for someone with British roots."

"I'm as Irish as anyone around here," Dessie snapped. "My granny was an O'Neill from County Cork, and my mother's family…" She stopped. Trying to explain the Irish-British links was a futile exercise. Irish history was too complex for the uninitiated. Nobody who hadn't grown up in Ireland would understand the relationship between the Irish and Anglo-Irish. She didn't even understand it herself, except for a deep feeling of belonging to this country, rather than to Britain. "There's more to the Irish than you might think," she said instead.

"I can see that," Marcus replied. "Sorry if I stepped on a sore toe."

"No problem." Dessie scanned the dark lane ahead for the first sight of the entrance to Killybeg House. She jumped as two pinpricks of light suddenly came into view. A dark shape stopped for a moment before it slunk into the shadows on the other side of the road,

Marcus stood on the brakes, and the car slewed sideways and stopped. "A bloody fox," he wheezed. "Sorry about that. It was a big bastard too. I could only see the lights reflected in the eyes at first, but then he was there, standing in the middle of the road, staring at us. Did you see him?"

"Just a glimpse. But he was big."

Marcus put the car into gear again and straightened the wheel. "Lots of foxes around here then?"

"Yes. Used to be anyway."

"Good fox hunting, I've heard. The Cloughmichael pack is famous for its great country. I mean the land they hunt over."

Dessie shrugged. "I suppose. I wouldn't know. I'm not into fox hunting. Or any kind of hunting. I'm not too fond of the idea of killing innocent animals for sport."

Marcus was about to answer but slowed down as the entrance came into view. He pulled up and looked in awe at the stone pillars and the arch above the black iron gates, where two granite wolfhounds stared haughtily down at them. "Wow," he mumbled. "They're beautiful."

"Brian Boru and Cú Chulainn," Dessie said. "One named after Brian Boru, a high king of Ireland, the other after a mythological hero. The dogs are supposed to have saved Michael O'Connor from drowning in eighteen-something. The hounds, I mean," she added as an afterthought. Why did she feel she had to explain everything to him?

"O'Connor?" Marcus asked, his eyes still on the wolf-hounds. "The guy who bought the house from the first owner?"

"That's right. You have a good memory."

Marcus turned and winked at Dessie. "I'm not just a pretty face, you know."

"Yeah, right. Please drive up to the house, if you don't mind. I'm sure the old housekeeper is waiting. I don't want to hold her up. She might want to go to bed early."

"It's not that late, but okay. She probably wants supper early so she can curl up in front of the TV with her cat."

"How do you know she has one?"

"Old women always do. Or a yappy little lapdog."

"I bet it's a cat."

"And I'd put my money on the little dog with a name like Toby or something."

Dessie laughed. "Okay. You're on. What will you give me if you lose?"

Gravel crunched under the wheels, and the car drew up in front of the dark shape of a cottage.

"We're here. The gate lodge." Marcus engaged the hand-brake. His eyes glittered in the light of the dashboard as he looked at Dessie. "What will I give you if I lose? I don't think you'd like what I have in mind, so let's just say the loser has to pay for dinner in a nice restaurant. How's that?"

"Deal." The look in his eyes told her a different story from his bland words, and Dessie felt her face flush, relieved it was too dark for him to notice.

The light over the red front door suddenly came on, and they scrambled to get out of the car. "Now we'll see," Marcus said. "I bet the old girl has the dog there in the hall."

"Or cat," Dessie hissed back as they walked up the granite steps.

The door opened, and the shape of a tall, slim woman came into view. A voice with a surprisingly young timbre called out to them. "There you are! I expected you hours ago. Where the feck have you been?"

Dessie's eyes widened when she could see clearly as they entered the brightly lit hall. The person before them was no elderly lady, but a very attractive young woman, with blonde hair cascading down her back and endless legs encased in skinny jeans. She held out her hand. "Hi. I'm Audrey. Welcome to Killybeg gate lodge."

CHAPTER 3

Dessie couldn't help staring at the woman. She didn't look much older than thirty, but she oozed confidence and a kind of quiet intelligence. Mesmerised, Dessie shook her hand. "Hi, Audrey. I'm Dessie." She could feel Marcus stiffen beside her and saw that he was just as stunned.

"I'll be..." he mumbled. "You're not at all what we expected." He held out his hand. "Marcus Smythe. Director of—"

"Smythe's Auctioneers." Audrey laughed. "Yeah, I know who you are." She shook his hand. "Hi there."

"Hi, Audrey." Marcus held on to her hand. "Miss Broadbent is my assistant."

"I know." Audrey nodded. "I had an e-mail from the managing director of your firm—your dad, right?"

Marcus nodded. "Yes. It's a family firm."

"I'm not really anyone's assistant," Dessie cut in. "I'm a trainee at the firm, and I was given this assignment because I know about Irish houses and art in Ireland during this period."

Audrey looked appraisingly at her. "Is that a Tipperary accent I hear? You from around here? You look like someone, but I can't quite figure out..."

Dessie hesitated. "I grew up in Cloughmichael."

"At the vicarage," Marcus interjected.

"The vicarage? There is no—" Audrey's eyes lit up, and she pointed at Dessie. "Yes! Now I know. You're Miranda's lost sister! You're the spit of her. Jesus, that's a hoot. Does she know you're back? And Jules? Have you told her?"

"No. Not yet," Dessie mumbled. She looked at Audrey. "Have they said anything about me?"

"Not much. Just that they have a sister who disappeared and never let them know where she went. There was some kind of…disagreement, they said. But that's all."

Dessie let out a sigh. "Oh. Good. Thank you."

"No bother," Audrey chortled. She looked past them into the dark night. "You have luggage? Better bring it in. It's going to lash in a minute."

"I only have a suitcase," Dessie replied. "But Marcus has a ton of luggage. You'd think he was moving here."

Marcus shot Dessie an annoyed glance. "Just some sports equipment. I intend to do some hiking while I'm here."

"And riding and fishing and shooting," Dessie quipped. "Wasn't that what you said?"

"Golf too? There are some excellent golf courses in this area," Audrey said, her eyes full of laughter.

Marcus walked back to the door. "No. I don't play golf. Terribly middle-aged and middle class, don't you think?"

"Oh, suuure," Audrey said and made a face behind his back at Dessie. "My boyfriend plays golf. Must tell him how middle class it is. He'll be devastated."

Marcus turned and looked at her. "I'm sorry. Actually, my father plays golf. Didn't meant to…"

Audrey flicked her hand at him. "Nah, I was only joking. I don't have a boyfriend."

Marcus shot her a dazzling smile. "Now, that's *very* good news."

Audrey's eyes turned cold. "Really? Must say that is a most unprofessional remark. But never mind. Go and get the luggage and join us in the kitchen when you've got it all inside. Come on, Dessie, I've opened a bottle of excellent plonk, and the steaks are sizzling. How do you like yours?"

"Medium rare," Marcus said.

Audrey glanced at him. "Oh, you're still there? I wouldn't hang around if I were you. All that sports equipment might get wet."

Dessie let out a giggle. This woman had the kind of sass she would love to possess. Dessie followed her into the kitchen and looked around in surprise. Not only warm and bright, it was like something out of *House & Home*, with Shaker-style cupboards, granite-top counters, and a state-of-the-art oven and ceramic hob. "This house must have been done up recently," she remarked.

"Yes." Audrey walked to the hob and put a large grill pan on one of the rings. "Only just finished. This is going to be one of the luxury cottages for rent when the big house is turned into a boutique hotel and spa."

"Oh. I had no idea."

"Nobody knows yet, so keep it to yourself. I only got this information while I was sniffing around, trying to find out the story of the house and the family. They've been gone for so long and now this. We'll be doing a big exposé in the local newspaper before Christmas about the auction and the future of the house."

"I see." Dessie sat down at the round oak table in the nook by the window. "It must be hard to look after that big house and edit the newspaper as well."

Audrey shrugged. "Not really. I had nowhere to stay when I came here a year ago, so when I saw the ad for manager of the property in return for free lodging at this house, I looked into what it would involve. There wasn't much to do, apart from supervising the cleaning staff that comes here once every two months to dust and hoover and to make sure the heating is turned to a low temperature during the winter months. That, and airing it regularly, is all I have to do. And then I get to live in this cute house. Don't know what I'll do when it's all sold, but I should have found something to rent by then."

"I'm sure you will."

Audrey poured wine into a glass and put it in front of Dessie. "Here. Nice little Beaujolais I found in Lidl. Don't tell snooty face. He'll only wrinkle his nose and tell us all about wine."

Dessie laughed. "He's not that bad. I have a feeling he's actually a little out of his depth here. Nice guy behind it all, I'd say."

"He'd be hot, if he weren't so uptight and superior. But maybe we can get him to relax."

Dessie shrugged. "Nah. Let's make him stew for a while."

Audrey laughed and was about to answer when Marcus walked in.

He took off his trench coat and hung it over a chair. "I left everything in the hall, as I don't quite know where the bedrooms are."

Audrey nodded. "The steaks are done. All medium rare. There are baked potatoes in the oven and grilled tomatoes too. Then salad with walnuts and Cashel Blue."

"Gosh," Dessie said. "It's like a five-star restaurant."

Audrey took the potatoes out of the oven. "I love cooking. It's so relaxing."

"Me too," Marcus said. "I love this kitchen. I had no idea I'd see something like this in rural Ireland."

"You'd be surprised how modern we are around here. We even have flush toilets and hot water." Audrey handed Marcus the dish. "Here, put this on the table, and I'll plate up the steaks. Do you want a little garlic butter on yours?"

"Yes, please," Marcus said meekly and went to join Dessie at the table.

Audrey arrived with the steaks. "Help yourself to wine."

Dessie attacked her steak while Marcus and Audrey

chatted. Stress always made her hungry. The mere mention of her sisters, Miranda and Juliet, had shaken her, and she realised she'd have to contact them as soon as she could. It wouldn't do for them to learn of her arrival from someone else, especially not Audrey, who, she suspected, was fond of gossip. But she was a journalist, after all, so that was probably part of her job.

"Riding, eh?" Audrey said, jolting Dessie out of her musings. "I suppose you'll want to do some fox hunting, then? Very popular around here. There are several packs, but the Cloughmichael one would be best suited to you. Very upmarket."

Marcus drained his glass. "Yes. I've already contacted them. I'm riding in the opening meet on Monday. They've booked a horse for me too."

Audrey nodded. "Good choice. They have the best horses, I've heard."

"I hope the horse is not the kind that would buck me off at the first covert," Marcus said.

Audrey looked confused. "Covert? What's that? I've heard the word, but I'm not into hunting, so…"

"A covert is a thicket, or woods, where the fox is likely to hide," Marcus explained.

Audrey nodded. "That's it. Thank you. But I don't think your hired horse will throw you off if it sees a fox. Especially if it's one of Jules'. Her hirelings are the best."

Dessie blinked. "Jules? You mean my sister? I didn't know she did hirelings."

"She only started last season," Audrey replied. "She let the land to Rory, and now all she has is twenty acres for the horses, so she got into hiring them out to visitors. Quite good money, she says, even if it's a lot of hard work."

"Good money indeed," Marcus cut in. "A hundred and twenty a day for the horse. Then a hundred that the hunt charges for the cap. Not a sport for the poor."

Audrey winked at him. "Yeah, but that keeps the riff-raff away, doesn't it?"

Marcus smiled. "Absolutely. I'd pay anything to do some real hunting here. In England, sadly, we're not allowed to chase foxes. We can only drag hunt."

"Officially, yeah," Audrey teased. "But I hear they hunt real foxes over there despite the ban."

"Stop it!" Dessie exclaimed. "I hate fox hunting. If they banned it here, I'd be over the moon. Hunting down and killing a beautiful animal for sport? How horrible."

Audrey and Marcus stared at her then looked at each other in what Dessie felt was a silent conspiracy, as if she were a child who didn't know better.

Marcus let his knife and fork fall on his plate with a clatter. "You have that Disney-cute-animal-idea, I gather. But foxes are vermin. They kill for sport themselves. Have you ever seen a henhouse after a fox has been in there? Dead hens scattered all over the place. And they go in and kill newborn lambs too."

Dessie glared at him. "That's just an excuse. What do you know about chickens and lambs? You just want to ride out on a good horse and jump fences and gallop through great countryside and then go and have a drink and a laugh in the pub afterwards. Boasting about the big fences you jumped," she ended.

Marcus looked at his plate then back at Dessie. "I don't deny what you just said. There is nothing more thrilling than a day's hunting on a good horse. But—"

"Hang on a second," Audrey cut in. "There is a lot more to hunting than you think. You grew up here, so you must know that everything revolves around fox hunting in rural Ireland in the winter. It's not all about hunting and killing a poor, cute little fox. Marcus is right. They are vermin. They need to be culled, and hunting is the best way to do that. If you knew about fox hunting, you would know that it's only the weak and old foxes that get killed. It's the survival of the fittest. This way, foxes get to grow stronger and healthier." Audrey took a swig of her wine. "But," she continued before Dessie had a chance to interrupt, "there is an awful lot more to it than that. There's a whole little industry around fox hunting. Horses are bred to hunt, saddlers make saddles for hunting, tack shops, blacksmiths, not to mention the breeding of the hounds and the hunt staff, are all there because of this ancient tradition. Thousands of people depend on fox hunting for their living."

"Yeah, but," Dessie interjected, "it's still a nasty way for an animal to die."

"I bet the foxes don't worry about that when they tear a rabbit apart alive," Marcus muttered.

"Oh, whatever. Let's drop it for now." Dessie pushed away her plate and sipped at her wine. "I'm really tired. If you could show me where my bedroom is, Audrey, I think I'll go to bed."

Audrey jumped up. "Of course. Follow me, and I'll get you sorted. What about you, Marcus?"

"I'll finish my steak and have some more wine. I'll catch up with you later, Audrey."

"I'm going out," Audrey said. "I have to check a few things in the office for tomorrow's edition. Then I'm meeting up with a few friends for a drink. But your room won't be hard to find. It's the only one upstairs. Dessie and I are in the two smaller rooms, downstairs."

Marcus nodded. "All right. I'll get myself organised."

Audrey pointed to the door at the other end of the kitchen. "You can put boots and stuff in the utility room in there. But make sure you don't upset Cat. She sleeps there."

Dessie laughed and winked at Marcus. "You have a cat?"

"More like she has me." Audrey laughed. "A black cat just wandered in here one evening and kind of told me she wanted to live here. So I adopted her. Don't know where she came from, but now she's mine. Or I'm hers. You know what cats are like."

"That's a lovely story," Dessie said. "Especially since it means you lose, Marcus."

"Lose what?" Audrey asked, looking mystified.

Dessie smiled. "We had a bet that you had either a dog or a cat. I said cat, so I won. Now Marcus has to take me out to dinner. Right, Marcus?"

Marcus nodded. "Of course. I'll have a look at restaurants in the area. Goodnight, Dessie. Sleep tight. We'll have to get started early tomorrow. I know it's Saturday, but I want to have a look at the house and draw up a schedule. Hope that's okay."

"Fine," Dessie replied. "I have no plans for the weekend. Except…"

"Except what?" Marcus enquired.

"Except getting in touch with my sisters. I'll do that later in the day, though. Not something I'm looking forward to."

Audrey stopped on her way to the door. "But won't they be happy to see you again? I mean, they thought you were gone forever, and now here you are, the long-lost baby sister. How great is that?"

Dessie sighed. "They won't exactly be shouting hallelujah, you know."

Audrey looked confused. "Why not?" She shrugged. "But that's none of my business, is it? Come on, let's get you settled so you can go to bed."

Dessie followed Audrey into the hall, picked up her suitcase and continued down a short corridor to the end, where Audrey threw a door open and switched on the light. Dessie discovered a cosy, country-cottage-style bedroom with a double bed, a chintz easy chair by the window, an antique chest of drawers and an old pine wardrobe. The wooden floorboards were partly covered by a rug in many colours, and there was a pretty lamp on the bedside table.

Chintz curtains matching the chair were drawn against the cold, wet night.

"What a lovely room," Dessie exclaimed.

"Yes. I think the decorators got it just right," Audrey replied. "But no en-suite, I'm afraid. We share a bathroom. Marcus has his own, though. Sorry about that, but I didn't fancy sharing a bathroom with a guy."

Dessie shuddered. "Especially that guy. I bet he spends hours just getting his hair done."

Audrey laughed. "Probably. Anyway, hope you get a good night's sleep. You can have the bathroom first. I'll probably be a bit late. There are towels on a shelf beside the bath. Yours are blue."

Dessie nodded. "Thanks. See you tomorrow."

After Audrey left, Dessie sank down on the bed and buried her face in her hands. She was here, finally. Back home in Cloughmichael. All through the evening, she had turned her mind away from the real issue, the conflict she was facing: contacting her sisters, especially Jules. How would she react when she heard Dessie was back? What would she say? Dessie hovered between holding on for a few days, and doing it at once, right then, that very moment. All she had to do was pick up the phone and say she was back. Dessie grabbed her bag and rooted for her phone. But when she found it, she put it back. No. Impossible. Not now. Maybe later. But a little voice inside her said, "Do it now, start the ball rolling." Dessie picked up the phone again and dialled the number she knew by heart, even after ten years. Her heart beat so fast she thought it would explode.

It rang once, twice, three times, then a voice: "Jules Thomas-Smith."

Dessie swallowed, cleared her dry throat. "Jules? It's me, Dessie. I'm…back."

CHAPTER 4

Silence. Dessie waited for Jules to hang up.

But then a shaky voice said, "Dessie? Oh, God. It can't be."

"It is," Dessie whispered. "It's me, and I'm here. Back in Cloughmichael. I need to see you."

"Are you in trouble?" Jules asked, her voice marginally stronger. "If you need money…"

"No!" Dessie shot up from the bed. "I'm fine. I'm here for a job. I wasn't going to call, but then I thought, what if you spotted me somewhere and had a heart attack or something…"

"Heart attack?" Jules snapped. "I'm not that old. What kind of job? Modelling?"

Dessie bristled. "Shit, don't you think I could handle something a bit more intelligent than modelling?" She swallowed, trying to keep her voice calm. "As a matter of fact, I have a degree in art history from Trinity. I'm now working for a well-known auctioneer in London, and they sent me here to catalogue Killybeg for the big auction at the end of December. That's why I'm here, not for some stupid modelling." Dessie fought an urge to stick out her tongue at the phone and hang up, but she held on. No need to act like a five-year-old.

"Does Miranda know?" Jules said at the other end.

"No. I rang you first. I only just arrived. I'm staying at the gatehouse with a woman called Audrey—"

"Yeah, yeah, I know her," Jules interrupted. "So you'll be here for a while, then?"

"At least until Christmas."

"Oh."

"Can I come and see you? I'd like to talk to you, to explain…"

Another long silence. "Explain?" Jules whispered. "Explain what? I don't think what you did can be explained."

"Yes, it can. It must be. I have to tell you that you were wrong, thinking I had…" Dessie couldn't get out the words. "Will you at least see me?" she whimpered, her eyes filling with tears.

"I'll think about it. You have to tell Miranda you're here."

"I will. I'm sure she'll give me a warmer welcome." Dessie hung up without saying goodbye. She lay down on the bed and let the tears come.

* * *

The room was flooded with light. Dessie stirred, opened her eyes, and sat up. She was stiff and sore, having fallen asleep with her clothes on. The half-drawn curtains let in the early morning sunshine, and the wind softly rattled the sash window that had been left open. Dessie checked her watch. Half past seven. Exhausted after all that had happened the day before, she had slept all night without waking up.

Cold and weary, Dessie undressed and put on the fluffy bathrobe hanging on the back of the door. She tiptoed into the little bathroom, where she found blue towels stacked on a shelf marked "Guests," along with an array of bath products, body lotions, exfoliating creams, and eau de cologne, all in sealed bottles, ready for use. She giggled, feeling she had died and gone to Harrods, turned on the shower, and stepped into the stream of warm water. She soaped herself all over with a large bar of French soap, its soft suds like whipped cream on her skin. Her hair was quickly shampooed and wrapped in a towel, and then she lathered body lotion all over, finishing with a light spray of Miss Dior.

Feeling like a new, much younger woman, she crept down the corridor, across the hall, and peered into the kitchen. Nobody there. Audrey might already have gone to work; Marcus was probably still asleep.

Dessie walked in and turned on the kettle, scouting around for bread, butter, and marmalade, which she found in the fridge. There was a rustle at the door of the utility room, and a black cat wandered in, meowing and winding herself between Dessie's legs. "You must be Cat." Dessie sat down at the table and lifted the cat on her lap. She helped herself to an apple from the fruit basket on the table, looking out at the avenue as she had her breakfast, the cat purring in her lap.

She could see all the way up to the front of the big house, where the pillared porch rose above a well-tended gravel drive. It seemed as if the house were slowly waking up from its long sleep. It looked much as it must have been in the early days, and Dessie conjured up images of ladies descending from carriages with the help of liveried footmen. What a graceful, elegant time it was, even if the dirt-poor Irish were starving outside the gates. She tried to imagine what it might have been like to be one of those ladies. Would she have noticed the poor and hungry? Would she have cared? Did they? As the vicar's daughter in the early eighteen hundreds, she might have been made aware of those less fortunate, of course, just as she and her sisters had been when they were children living in the vicarage.

Dessie's thoughts drifted to her childhood, those happy days before anything bad had happened. Three girls growing up in an old house, brought up by strict but loving parents who didn't have much money but who still managed to keep a certain style and class. They had lived frugally, but the girls received a rich education when it came to literature, music, and nature. Dessie sighed. Those were the good times, before Granny died, her mother only two years later, followed by her dad, leaving three young girls without a family. Then the vicarage was sold, as the Protestant Church of Ireland were cutting down on the clergy and abolishing smaller parishes. But by then they were grown up, or at least Miranda and Juliet were. Miranda looked after their baby sister when she was first married and her husband, Jerry, bought the vicarage. And Jules married Harry.

Oh, Harry… Dessie blinked away tears as she buttered yet another slice of toast. No use thinking about that—about *him* and what happened, and what hadn't, despite what everyone believed. It was all in the past.

The door opened. Startled, Dessie whipped around as Marcus, dressed in jeans and a black polo neck, strolled in. She clutched her bathrobe and gave him a polite smile. "Good morning. I thought you might still be asleep."

"Wide awake since seven. Morning, Dessie. Did you sleep well?" Marcus switched on the kettle.

"Yes, thank you."

"I see the cat appeared."

Dessie stroked the soft black fur. "Yes, this is Cat."

"A handsome cat."

"She is. But I'd better get dressed and dry my hair." Dessie pushed her plate aside, placed Cat on the floor, and got up.

"There's no rush. But I would like to head up to the house in about half an hour. Just to walk through it and decide on a plan. The light's good too, so it's a perfect time to have a look at everything."

Dessie nodded. "Of course. I'll see you in a minute. Audrey said to help ourselves to breakfast, but then we have to buy our own food. She only cooked dinner last night to help out as we had just arrived."

"Yes, I know. We can go to Clonmel to do our shopping later. I'd let you go on your own, but you don't have a car, so…"

Dessie frowned. "No, I don't. Maybe I should rent one? I forgot how you're stranded in the country if you don't have a car. I don't even think about it in London."

"It's more of a nuisance in the city. Are you finished with that teapot?"

"Yes. I had my breakfast. I was just sitting here daydreaming, really."

"About the good old days?"

"Maybe. See you in a little while." Dessie went back to her room to get dressed and quickly blow dry her hair. She had just put on her jeans, shirt, and warm sweater, when her phone rang.

She picked up on the second ring. "Hello?"

"Dessie, it's Miranda."

Dessie froze. "Oh. How did you…?"

"Jules. She rang last night sounding upset. She told me you were here and why and gave me your number."

"I see." Dessie tried to think of something to say. "How are you?"

"Fine, thanks."

"And Jerry and the boys?"

"Fine too. Dessie, I'd like to see you. Can you come to the house? Maybe this evening? Jerry's away, and the boys are at a weekend scout camp, so I thought…"

"That it would be a good time as nobody would see me?" Dessie tried to keep the bitterness out of her voice.

"No," Miranda said softly. "Not really that, but I thought it would be good to talk. Just you and me. Would that be okay?"

Dessie considered Miranda's suggestion. It would be

hard to meet again, but Miranda had always been more for-giving and understanding than Jules, who always jumped to the wrong conclusions—usually bad. Miranda always gave you the benefit of the doubt. She *listened.* "Yes. That would be okay," Dessie replied. "But only if you…" She stopped. "I have so much I want to tell you."

Miranda let out a long sigh. "Wonderful. I was afraid you wouldn't…oh, I don't know what I was afraid of. But one step at a time, right? Let's go slowly."

"Yes. That's what we should do." Dessie relaxed. It would be okay. It would be good to talk to Miranda. "See you tonight. I have to go. We—this director I'm working for and I—have to go and see the house now."

"The house? Won't that be a bit spooky?"

"I suppose," Dessie said. "No one has lived there for so long. There are bound to be echoes of times past." *Like ripping a plaster off a deep wound*, she thought. *But it has to be done. So I can start to heal.*

"Probably," Miranda said. "But it'll be exciting too. Take care, Dessie. Don't let the ghosts get to you."

"I won't," Dessie replied, thinking that Miranda had, without knowing it, voiced the fears that had haunted her for so long.

* * *

The ghosts, Dessie thought as they walked up the long, tree-lined avenue to the big house on the hill. *The ghosts of a summer past…* She tried her best to keep up with Marcus' long strides while she steeled herself to what it would feel like to push that heavy front door open and step into the hall, smelling the musty odour of the house that had always prevailed, despite airing and cleaning.

Marcus turned and looked at her. "Are you okay? Come

along, we don't have much time before the clouds roll in. I want to see everything in this bright sunlight."

"I'm coming," Dessie panted. "But you're walking so fast, I have to run."

"Not very fit, are we?" Marcus teased.

Dessie half-ran to his side. "I'm very fit, actually. I walk a lot and go to the gym and do yoga twice a week," she continued, wondering why she felt she had to prove anything to him.

"Yoga?" he scoffed. "That's not what I call a sport. Doesn't make you very fit, does it?"

"Yoga is not a sport as such, no. But it's very challenging. I'd like to see you balance on one leg and stay there for longer than a few seconds. Not to mention a lot of the other poses that take years to master. Yoga gives you everything: strength, suppleness, flexibility, and balance. I don't know any form of exercise that is more complete."

"Except it doesn't improve your cardio fitness." Marcus slowed his walk.

"No, and that's why I do a lot of walking."

Marcus looked down at her, a smile hovering on his lips. "And hiking?"

"I do hillwalking when I can. I've been to Scotland and the Lake District with a few friends. We try to get away when we have days off or during long weekends," Dessie said primly.

"Sounds like the perfect fitness regime." Marcus' gaze skimmed her body. "Explains your lithe and supple frame."

Dessie glared at him. "Thanks, if that was supposed to be a compliment."

"Just stating a fact, that's all. God forbid I pay you a compliment. That would be sexual harassment, wouldn't it?"

"Depends." Dessie looked up at him. "But if we're working together, I suggest we keep compliments or anything else personal to a minimum."

"Absolutely," Marcus said, that little smile still making his mouth quiver. "We have to stay professional, don't we?"

Dessie was about to shoot him a snippy reply, but they had arrived at the house and the sight of it silenced her.

"It's some house," Marcus said as they stood there looking up at the portico. "So graceful, yet imposing. The Georgians sure knew how to build."

"They took their inspiration from the Palladian style in Italy in the Middle Ages," Dessie mumbled.

"Venice," Marcus corrected. "It wasn't Italy then."

Dessie nodded. "Yes, sorry. That's right. Actually, Palladio was inspired by the style of ancient Greece, I read somewhere."

Marcus nodded. "Yes. This house is in good nick. Just look at the bay windows. I wonder if that's—"

"The drawing room," Dessie filled in. "It has glorious views of the valley and mountains beyond."

Marcus looked at her. "You've been in this house?"

Dessie squirmed. "Yes. Once. Years ago. Someone took me for a tour."

"I see." Marcus took a bunch of keys from the pocket of his trench coat. "Okay, let's go and have a look, then. You can lead the way, as you know the house so well."

"I haven't been here for years. Can't remember much about it," Dessie protested.

"Yes, whatever." Marcus walked up the wide granite steps to the entrance, inserted the biggest key into the huge lock, and gave it a strong twist. The lock clicked. Marcus pushed against the door, and it swung open silently. "Very well oiled, I have to say." He stood aside and made a pretend bow. "After you, princess."

Dessie shivered, her throat constricting. She took a deep breath, climbed the steps, her legs like jelly, and hesitated for a moment on the doorstep. Then she walked into the house and back in time to that day over ten years earlier.

CHAPTER 5

The big hall was flooded with light. Dessie looked up at the intricately carved staircase rising all the way to the third floor, where a glass dome let in the sunlight. "How beautiful," she breathed. "It's like looking into heaven."

Richard put his hand on her shoulder. "I've always loved this hall."

"Thank you for showing it to me."

Richard laughed. "There's a lot more to see than the entrance." He took her hand. "Come on, let's do the grand tour."

Dessie hesitated. "Are you sure it's all right? Won't we get into trouble being here like this without permission?"

"It's fine. My dad and his aunt own the place now, and he told me to come here and check the house to make sure no windows are open or that anyone left a light on. I'm trying to get someone to keep an eye on it when I leave. This is a great opportunity to have a good ol' snoop around."

"Okay." Dessie let herself be pulled along. They tiptoed across the beautiful oriental carpet and down a corridor lined with paintings, sculptures, and carved consoles that Richard told her originated in China, brought home by one of his ancestors after his long posting there during the days of the British Empire. Dessie's pale face was reflected in the huge gold-framed mirrors, and their footsteps on the parquet floor echoed eerily through the vast, musty rooms. They walked through a cavernous drawing room furnished with antique sofas and chairs, mahogany occasional tables and padded footstools. The floor was covered with another oriental carpet still in mint condition, the pattern of deep red, green and gold gleaming in the light from the French windows that overlooked stunning views of the valley and mountains beyond.

Dessie stopped in front of a table with an array of photographs in silver frames. "Is this them? Your ancestors?"

"Yes." Richard picked up one of the photos. "Here he is. Tom Hourigan. My great-granddad."

Dessie peered at a black-and-white photo of a pale young man in a dark suit. "Not very like you. He looks so solemn."

"They all did in those days. He was just about to depart to India to work as an engineer. Didn't come back until thirty years later after his parents died. Then he married a Spanish girl called Conchita. She was supposed to have been very beautiful."

"Is that where you got your black hair and olive skin?" Dessie enquired.

Richard laughed. "I suppose. And my blue eyes are from my Irish ancestors."

"Why did the family move to America?"

Richard put the photo back on the table. "Conchita upped and left in 1936 to fight in the Spanish Civil War. She was a socialist and a patriot. She wanted to help free her country from the right-wing regime. Sadly, she died during an air raid in Andalucía. Then my great-grandad didn't want to live here anymore, so he closed up the house and took the children, my grandad and my great-aunt Rose, to live in New York, where he started a business. My grandfather married an Irish girl and went into law, and my dad followed in his footsteps. The house was left unoccupied all this time. Neither my dad nor my great-aunt want to sell it. I think they both feel some kind of connection with the old country and this is the only link to it. My dad is even thinking of retiring here. Until then, it'll be sitting empty, like some kind of museum. Expensive, but they can afford it."

"What about you?" Dessie asked, puzzled by the disdain in his eyes. "Do you want to live here when it's yours?"

Richard laughed. "No, sweetheart, I don't. I couldn't live in Ireland. Especially not in the depth of the Irish country-side. I will have a career in my dad's law firm, and then I will take over when the time comes. I have to think of my future wife too. She isn't exactly what you'd call a country girl. We'll be living in New York and have a weekend place in Connecticut. The all-American lifestyle." He pulled her close. "But I'll always have a soft spot for my Irish colleen."

Dessie pulled away. She was deeply in love with him, had been all summer, but she didn't like his condescending tone. She knew she was just his summer fling, his final flirt before he married Stacey or Courtney or whatever that posh girl in New York was called. "I'm no colleen," she protested.

"I forget." He laughed. "You're the vicar's daughter. Remnant of the British Empire. But brought up in Ireland. Must make you feel confused."

"In a way. When I'm with people like you. But not with the people I grew up with. My roots are in Ireland. My dad always said that we're part of the rich patchwork that makes up this country. British, Irish, Norman, and Viking—they're all there in every Irish man or woman. My granny was an O'Neill from County Cork. My mum is from an old Norman family. In any case, you're Irish too, despite that American accent." She drew breath and looked away from his teasing smile and twinkling eyes. "Can we go and see the rest of the house now?"

"Yes, my darling. Maybe you'd like to see the bedrooms?"

She blushed, knowing what he meant. But she wasn't going to give in, despite his hot looks and flirtatious ways.

She would have been ready to take that final step if he didn't keep mentioning his fiancée in New York. It was like being wooed by a married man. Kissing and cuddling was bad enough, sleeping with him would be the ultimate sin. "Let's see the library," she suggested.

"Yes, miss prim and proper. When are you going to join the twenty-first century?" He pulled her close again. "Don't tell me you don't want what I want. I can see it in your eyes."

She broke away from his hot breath on her face, his warm hands on her bare arms, and the scent of his aftershave. "Not now, Richard. Not here."

There was a glint of hope in his eyes. "But somewhere else? Soon?"

"Maybe." She laughed and skipped across the carpet. "Right now, I want you to show me the rest of the house." She wanted to distract him, to make him think of something else instead of constantly trying to seduce her. She was, at only nineteen, too young to handle a sexual relationship, even if her hormones had other ideas. She wanted him—oh God, yes—but was frightened of sex. It would be painful and scary, pulling her into something she wouldn't be able to cope with. And what if she got pregnant? Then he'd abandon her and run to New York and his fiancée.

The summer had been like a beautiful dream from which she didn't want to wake up. Meeting Richard secretly at the lake for picnics, going on long hikes in the mountains, and riding along the river on the land that belonged to Killybeg, on horses borrowed from Harry, her brother-in-law. It had all been like something from one of the romance novels she loved. But no sex, not yet. She wanted the romance to go on this way, not descend into something sleazy that she'd regret for the rest of her life.

They continued their tour, forgetting their feelings, mesmerised by the elegance and beauty of the house, the many paintings by famous artists of the eighteenth and nineteenth centuries, the exquisite collections of china and glassware and the jewel colours of the carpets and tapestries.

"What a wonderful house," Dessie sighed, looking again up the staircase rising gracefully to the glass dome above. "Can we go upstairs?"

"Of course." Richard walked up the stairs, Dessie in tow. "I've never seen the bedrooms, but I've heard they're magnificent."

He was both right and wrong. The bedrooms were all lavishly furnished, but the beds had been stripped of their mattresses and the curtains removed from the four posters. They quickly moved through bedrooms that echoed with thin whispers of sadness and despair.

Dessie stopped at the door of a large room, unable to enter. "Oh," she whispered and pointed at a collection of dolls lined up on a small bed. "It's the nursery. Look, there's a rocking horse and a doll's pram…" She was suddenly over-whelmed with a melancholy she couldn't explain. "Let's go," she said over her shoulder to Richard, who was coming out of another room down the corridor.

"Why? We haven't seen everything yet."

"I've seen enough." She closed the door to the nursery and started to walk down the long gallery toward the stairs. "It feels kind of spooky and cold here. I need to get out into the sunshine. Maybe we can have a look at the walled garden?"

"Yes, you're right. I get this eerie feeling someone's watching us." He shivered, smiling apologetically. "Probably my imagination, but I have a feeling the ghosts of the former occupants are floating around and don't want us up here."

They ran down the stairs and out the door, slamming it shut. "Phew." Richard turned his face to the sun. "That was weird. It's good to be outside in God's fresh air." He looked happy and carefree standing on the steps of his ancestral home, as if he belonged there.

"Maybe you should move here when you inherit this place?" Dessie suggested.

He opened his eyes and smiled at her. "I told you I never could, didn't I? In any case, that's a lifetime away. I want to live my life, not wait for someone else to die before I get an old house."

"And when you do, will you sell it?"

He shrugged. "Probably. But I'm too young to worry about the distant future." He skipped down the steps. "Come on, let's see the walled garden. I'm sure it's enchanting in this lovely sunshine."

Dessie laughed and followed him. It was a beautiful day. She was young and pretty and in love with this gorgeous man. So he was engaged. Engaged wasn't married. He was in love with her he said; he wanted her. She wanted him too. Maybe, if she gave him what he wanted most, he'd ditch that girl in New York and decide Dessie was his true love?

She went through the arch in the old stone wall that led to the walled garden and stopped, enchanted. "What a beautiful place," she exclaimed.

Richard looked around, as if he had just noticed the rose bushes heavy with blooms in a riot of colours, the gnarled apple and plum trees, their branches weighed down with fruit, the old walls covered in ivy, and more roses climbing all the way to the top. The still air was full of the scent of flowers and ripening fruit. A thrush serenaded them from the top of a monkey puzzle tree, and bees buzzed, moving from flower to flower.

Richard sighed and sank down on the grass. "Ah, August. My favourite month. Especially on a day like today. Isn't it grand?"

She sat down on the grass beside him, laughing. "Oh, yes. It's incredibly grand."

He put his arms around her and pulled her close. "And romantic? I feel very romantic right now. Don't you?"

She looked into his twinkling eyes. "Yes, I do," she whispered.

He kissed her lightly on the lips. "And something else, too?"

"Maybe," she mumbled, her mouth against his.

He kissed her harder, making her open her mouth and tasting his tongue. "Oh, baby. My darling, sweet Dessie…I love you."

She blinked, afraid to move. "You do? Really? You love me?"

He looked deep into her eyes. "Yes. Dessie, I have tried not to, but I can't help it. I have fallen in love with you."

That was it. What she had waited for all summer. "I love you too," she whispered, knowing there was no going back. "I love you so much, Richard."

He lay down, pulling her on top of him, kissing her, his mouth moving from her lips to her neck, then the swell of her breasts under the thin summer dress. He ran his hands down her body, to her thighs, pulling up her skirt, then rolling them both over so he was on top and her back was pressed into the damp grass. "Dessie, you're my girl," he said. "I can't stand it much longer. Please don't make me wait anymore."

She closed her eyes, frightened of the intensity of his voice and his hot gaze. "I won't."

"You want it too, don't you?" he mumbled into her ear, breathing hard.

"Yes," she whispered and pulled him tighter against her, parting her legs without thinking, the danger suddenly exciting rather than frightening. "I want you, Richard."

"Now?" He asked, his hand between her thighs.

"Yes. Now," she panted, hot desire pulsing through her. She suddenly couldn't control herself and acted out of some deep instinct, moving, arching her hips. Doing everything he wanted even before he asked.

Afterwards, she lay still, tears seeping out of her closed eyes.

He touched her face. "Baby, you're wonderful. Was it the first time? Did I hurt you?"

She smiled and opened her eyes. "Yes, it hurt a bit but then…something happened. It was like a slow explosion. Like fireworks."

"Next time it will be better, I swear."

"Better than this? How could it be? I don't know what happened, but it was glorious."

He sat up. "You had an orgasm, sweetheart. That's good. Do you know how good that is?" He sounded like teacher with a child who had performed well in an exam.

"It felt amazing." She watched him as he zipped up his trousers while she pulled the skirt of her dress over her legs. She didn't feel ashamed. It was right and good. They were in love. Richard would leave his fiancée and marry her. She closed her eyes to the afternoon sun and started to plan their wedding. They would be married in the pretty little Protestant church in Clonmel. Harry might walk her up the aisle, as Dad had passed away two years ago. Miranda would be matron of honour, Jules' little boy ring bearer…

"I have to go," Richard said, cutting into her daydream. "I have to call my dad. Organise my trip back. Lots to tell him. Then I have to speak to the people who manage the property and see if there are things to discuss. Like the heating and the cleaning schedule. The house has to be aired and dusted regularly and checked for damage from wind and rain. After all, that's why I'm here. I've been a little lax about such things. You were too much of a distraction, my sweet."

She grinned. "I'm sorry. But it wasn't on purpose. It just happened, didn't it?"

He laughed. "Yeah, you just kinda happened to be there, at the country market, looking like my dream girl with your huge dark eyes, silky black hair, and long brown legs."

She giggled. "You didn't have to talk to me. I could have just brushed past you and walked away."

He pulled her up and ran his hands over her bare arms. "How? It wouldn't be possible to see you and not talk to you. And then you said 'Hello' and 'How are you?' and 'What are you doing in this little town?' in that lilting Irish accent, and I was hooked."

"Me too," she breathed, pressing her face against his chest. "Hooked on you."

"You have grass stains on your dress."

"I don't care."

"But how will you explain if your sisters see them?"

Dessie shrugged. "Miranda? She won't notice. She's so busy with the boys and the farm and Jerry, she hardly has time to say hello. Juliet wouldn't notice much either. She's only interested in horses and dogs. Nobody pays much attention to me."

Richard nodded. "Good." He let go of her and ran his hand through his brown hair. "So long then, babe. Must run. I'll see you before I go back, I hope."

Dessie laughed. "Of course you will. We have to make plans, don't we?"

He kissed her cheek. "Sure. We'll make plans. Soon. Cheers for now."

"Cheers," Dessie mumbled. She watched his tall figure as he walked through the archway and disappeared. She never saw him again.

CHAPTER 6

The old vicarage looked exactly the same as it had ten years earlier, except for the mountain ash by the gate, which had grown from a mere sapling to a tall tree. Dessie pushed the gate open and walked up the stone-flagged path to the red front door. She hesitated, straightening her back, clearing her dry throat before she rang the doorbell. The chimes were the same as before, echoing inside, where she knew the hall would be crammed with coats, jackets, and boots, the old refectory table covered in letters and newspapers and the lamp with the red shade casting a warm glow on oak-panelled walls and the old print of Queen Victoria.

A few drops of rain spattered against the windows. Dessie hoped Miranda would open the door before the rain turned heavy. A shadow appeared through the pane, then Miranda flung the door open and they stood looking at each other for a full minute.

"Dessie," Miranda mumbled and pulled her into the hall, where they burst into tears and fell into each other's arms, the door swinging shut in a sudden gust of wind.

Dessie hugged Miranda and breathed in her familiar spicy perfume. She pulled back and wiped her eyes with her hand, staring at her older sister. Apart from a few laughter lines around her eyes and a slightly thinner frame, Miranda hadn't changed much. "You look the same," Dessie said.

"How weird."

Miranda laughed and wiped her tears away with the sleeve of her multicoloured tunic. "What did you expect? White hair and a wooden leg? I'm only thirty-eight, for God's sake. But look at you. All grown up and gorgeous. I love that green jacket." Her gaze scanned Dessie from head to toe. "The boots are divine. All this from London?"

"Yes. I love shopping there. But with my puny salary, I have to buy things during the sales."

"No one would guess. You look so glamorous."

"Thank you."

"But come in. I made a chicken casserole. You know, the one with cream and herbs that you used to love."

"Lovely. I'm starving. I didn't eat yet. I knew you'd be cooking up a storm. I bet you baked bread, and there is an apple pie lurking in the fridge."

Miranda laughed and led the way through the comfortable living room to the big farmhouse kitchen, where an AGA stove emitted cosy warmth and delicious smells of chicken casserole and newly baked bread. "No apple pie, I'm afraid. The boys demolished it before they left. You have no idea the amount of food three boys can put away in a very short time."

"Lucky for them their mum is an ace cook." Dessie sat down at the pine table and ran her hands lovingly over the scarred surface. She had sat there many long winter evenings doing her homework while Granny sat at the other end, sewing or knitting, her cat purring in her lap and the radio playing Irish ballads.

Miranda put a steaming plate piled with chicken, potatoes, and runner beans in front of Dessie. "There you go. Eat up. You need a little fattening."

Dessie laughed and picked up a fork. "Look who's talking. You're like a greyhound yourself."

Miranda helped herself from the pots on the stove and

joined Dessie at the table. "I know. It's all the running around with the boys and the work at the farm. I never seem to get a chance to sit down."

"The farm? You mean you're still doing all that organic stuff?"

Miranda nodded and put a forkful of food in her mouth. "Yeah, and we're opening our new shop just before Christmas. Organically grown apples, pears, and vegetables. I'm also making jams and preserves. I'm going to start a website and sell online."

Dessie stared at her. "All by yourself?"

"No, Jerry's working with me now," Miranda replied. "His publishing business went belly-up last year, so he joined forces with me and now we're doing this together."

"His publishing business failed? What about the newspaper? Is that gone too?"

Miranda shook her head. "No, that's going very well. Ever since Finola McGee blew in like a tornado and changed things around, The Knockmealdown News has been selling like hotcakes. It was all due to Finola and that movie that was made here last year. Not to mention her whirlwind romance with Colin Foley and their secret wedding." Miranda sighed. "Ah, Finola. What a woman. And now she's had twins and they're living in LA, and she's writing those controversial articles about the presidential election over there. I'm sure you've read them in The Irish Times."

"Oh, yes. I love them. Her last one caused a huge Twitter storm. She doesn't mince her words." Dessie shoved a huge forkful of potatoes and sauce into her mouth. "Oh God, this is good," she mumbled through her mouthful.

"I knew you'd love it."

Dessie swallowed and wiped her mouth. "I missed the excitement last year, but I read all about it. I still have that magazine about the movie they produced."

Miranda laughed. "The magazine did a lot better than the movie. All due to Finola, of course. She's magic."

"I'd love to meet her."

"You might get the chance. Jules said they're thinking of coming here for Christmas. They still have the lease on the cottage."

Dessie's heart sank at the mention of their sister. She put down her fork. "I'm not sure I'll be here for Christmas. The auction is just before the holidays, and then I'll be going back to London."

Miranda topped up Dessie's glass with water from a blue jug. "Going back to what, exactly?"

Dessie shrugged. "Back to the flat I share with two career bitches. I have friends, but they'll be going home for Christmas. No boyfriend to speak of, except for a doctor I date sometimes. But he's not really a boyfriend. We're just a kind of desperate, lonely twosome. We go to the movies and sometimes to the pub. He comes with me if I need a date for a party, so I won't look so pathetic. We're each other's security net."

Miranda stared at Dessie. "I'd laugh if it weren't so sad. I don't understand what's going on here. Look at you—slim, pretty, and stylish. What's wrong with men in London?"

Dessie shrugged. "What's wrong with *me*, you mean. Men don't find me exactly fascinating. Maybe it's my aura. I exude hostility or something. I don't trust men. Maybe that's too obvious?"

Miranda looked thoughtful. "Is it? I haven't a clue. I'm not a man. But Jesus, Dessie, you were the most beautiful girl around here when you were younger. There wasn't a man in this county who didn't fancy you."

Dessie looked at her plate and pushed the remaining bits of chicken around. "I don't know what you mean." She looked up and met Miranda's eyes. "You know I left because of that awful rumour. The one about me and…Harry. It wasn't true. Breda Quirke saw something and drew the wrong conclusion. Then she ran around and told everybody."

Miranda shrugged. "No, not everybody. She just dropped a little bombshell in the pony club and the Tidy Towns Committee, and that got the ball rolling. Of course, as it was about the girl everyone wanted to be, the girl they were so jealous of, those small-town bitches lapped it all up. When it finally reached Jules, the story had been blown out of all proportions. What was probably just a friendly, brotherly hug, became full-on sex with a married man who happened to be your brother-in-law."

Dessie's shoulders slumped. "Yeah. That's all it was. A brotherly hug." Tears welled up as she looked at Miranda. "It wasn't him I was in love with, you know. Harry was just feeling sorry for me. I ran to the stables to hide when…that guy dumped me. Harry found me there, lying in the straw in an empty stall crying my eyes out. He lifted me up and held me. He didn't know what was going on. I didn't tell him. He didn't ask any questions. He just let me cry. Harry was always like a big brother to me. But Jules didn't believe me when I told her what had really happened."

"You told her about this other man?"

"No, just that I had been sad and Harry comforted me."

"Why didn't you tell me about that…that creep who dumped you?"

"I was too ashamed," Dessie mumbled.

Miranda frowned. "Ashamed? Why? Did you...?"

Dessie nodded. "Yeah. I did. It was the first time, and it was amazing." She looked defiantly at Miranda. "I never knew sex was that fantastic, but maybe I had the good fortune to fall for an expert."

"Who was he? Do I know him? Please don't tell me it's none of my business. I'm your sister, and I care about you."

Dessie shifted on the chair. "I want to tell you. It was Richard Hourigan."

Miranda's eyes widened. "Richard Hourigan? Who's… oh, you mean the owner of Killybeg?" She paused, looking puzzled. "But he…was he here that summer?"

Dessie laughed bitterly. "Was he here? Definitely."

Miranda nodded. "Oh, yes, I remember now. He was. We all met him at the country fair. And we all thought he was so hot. But how did you get together with him? I don't remember you going out with him, but that summer is a blur of babies and nappies. Three small children sure take your mind off what's going on in the world."

Dessie smiled. "Yeah, you sure were busy. So was Jules. Tony was only three that summer, and she had a lot of foals and young horses to break and school. Both she and Harry were up to their eyes."

"And then you and Richard had this love affair. Did he just dump you after that?"

Dessie wiped her eyes with her napkin. "Yeah. He went back to his fancy schmancy fiancée in New York."

"Bastard."

"I should have known better."

"Yes, but you were only nineteen," Miranda argued. "Jesus, what a creep. He took advantage of an innocent girl and then dumped her. You must have been devastated. I understand now what happened with Harry. But Jules probably wanted to believe the gossip. Their marriage was heading for the rocks at the time. It doesn't excuse her for not sticking up for you. If we had been more supportive, you wouldn't have had to leave. I've always felt guilty about that."

Dessie reached out and touched Miranda's hand. "There's no need to feel guilty. It all turned out well in the end. I would never have my degree or the job I have now if I hadn't left. It was hard at first, but it made me stronger. I'm okay. Better than if I'd stayed here and married some farmer." She suddenly giggled. "You know what? I had more fun as a slut than as the vicar's prim daughter. Those gossiping bitches decided I was a fallen woman, so I became one. What did I have to lose?"

Miranda choked on her last bite of chicken. "Slut?" she

wheezed when she got her breath back. "You mean you—"

"—screwed around?" Dessie grinned. "Yeah. Trinity College was a great place for that. There were some really sexy guys in my year. I dated most of them. Not all at the same time, though. I laid them end to end and made them last until I graduated." She sighed. "Those were the days. Wine, men, and song. Pretty exhausting too, as I had to hold down two jobs to pay my fees. I also had to take a student loan that I'm still paying off."

Miranda shook her head and sighed. "I can't believe what you just said. Tell me you were joking."

"Sorry. But no, I wasn't."

"I see." Miranda got up and started to clear the plates. "It'll take me a while to digest all of this." She stopped on her way to the dishwasher and smiled at Dessie. "But whatever you've been up to, it's great to have you back. I've missed you."

Dessie got up and put her arms around Miranda. "Me too. I missed you so much."

Miranda loaded the dishwasher while Dessie walked around the kitchen looking at photos and children's drawings pinned to the cork notice board on the wall. She ran her fingers over the pine worktops where her mother and grandmother and all the vicars' wives before them had prepared meals, baked buns, and made tea through the centuries since the house was built. The walls were infused with the scent of baking and cooking, and the air had a faint whiff of turf and woodsmoke from the stove that was still the warm, glowing heart of the house. "I love it," she mumbled.

"Love what?" Miranda asked, as she rummaged in a cupboard full of teacups and plates.

"This kitchen. It hasn't changed. I can still feel Mum's presence. And Granny's too."

Miranda put two cups and saucers on the counter and switched on the kettle. "Yes, they're still here, looking over my shoulder when I cook. It can be a bit overpowering at times. But it sure keeps me on my toes."

"I'm so glad Jerry bought this house when the parish was discontinued. I couldn't bear the thought of someone else living here."

"No. That would have been too sad." Miranda poured hot water into the teapot and put the tea things and a plate of cinnamon buns on a tray. "Let's have our tea in the living room. I'll light the fire."

Dessie was about to reply when she heard a knock on the back door. She stiffened as she stared at Miranda. "Someone's here. Could it be Jerry?"

Miranda put the tray on the counter. "He wouldn't knock."

"What are we going to do?"

"Open the door, of course." Miranda ran through the utility room and unlocked the back door. She paused for a moment, then Dessie heard her laugh. "Shit, you scared us! What are you doing here? Come in out of the rain, you eejit. You'll never guess who's here."

"Who?" a male voice asked.

"Come in and see for yourself. But take off that wet jacket first."

Dessie stared at the tall man coming into the kitchen. That reddish-brown hair and grey eyes gave her a shock of recognition. Oh, no. Not him.

He was the first to break the silence. "Holy Mother," he whispered, his face white. "It's you."

Dessie pulled herself together and smiled sweetly. "Yes, Rory. It's me. I've come back from the dead to haunt you."

"Jesus," he whispered, still staring at her. "I can't believe it."

Dessie turned to Miranda. "I'm suddenly not in the mood for tea by the fire. I think I'll go back to the gatehouse."

Miranda nodded. "I'll drive you." She glanced at Rory.

"Sorry, Rory, this isn't a good time. Did you call in to discuss something urgent?"

Rory shrugged. "No, I just wanted to go through the lease. You said you wanted those two acres near the paddocks?"

"Yes. I was going to give you a call about the lease. But right now…"

"Not the best moment for me either." Rory walked back to the utility room and left, banging the door shut behind him.

CHAPTER 7

Rory Quirke. Dessie clenched her jaw as Miranda drove her back to the gatehouse. His mother, Breda, was the source of the gossip that had spread like wildfire through the town. It wasn't long before everyone had heard the vile accusations, and Dessie had been forced to leave. She wasn't sure if Rory had helped spread the rumours, but he was Breda's son and could have stopped her or at least tried to defend Dessie. But he did nothing. *The coward*, she thought. *The spineless creep.*

Miranda pulled up in front of the gatehouse. "We're here."

Dessie snapped out of her thoughts. "Thank you for driving me back. I could have called a taxi."

"If you wanted to wait for an hour. We still only have one taxi. They're trying to get more. We need them badly. There'd be fewer drunk drivers if we had taxis to take the beer drinkers home from the pub."

"That's for sure. Do you want to come in? It's not too late, and I see a light on in the living room. Audrey must still be up."

Miranda touched Dessie's cheek. "No, not tonight. I think you should try to get to bed early. You look tired."

"You're right. I'll try to get some sleep. Even if meeting Rory will be etched into my brain for a while. Seeing him walking into your kitchen gave me such a jolt."

"Poor man. He hasn't had it easy."

"Still under his mother's thumb, then?"

"Not anymore. She finally moved out. She went to live with her sister in Dungarvan. I think it had something to do with her health problems."

Dessie brightened. "Health problems? I hope it's something embarrassing and painful."

Miranda had to laugh. "Yeah, me too. Not very Christian, but neither is she. I'm not sure what's wrong with her. Just arthritis and old age, I suspect. Plus the big showdown they had at the farm last year. Rory and one of his sisters had it out with Breda and gave her some kind of ultimatum. She went off in a huff, probably thinking Rory would beg her to come back, but she's still waiting. He's going around looking as if he's won the lottery. Now he can run his farm the way he wants without that woman butting in. Win-win for him."

"I bet he'll be getting married next, now that Breda isn't there to sneer at every woman who comes into the house."

"Hmm, yes. Maybe." Miranda stared into the dark night.

Dessie studied her. "What? You look as if you know something. There's a woman out there that Rory's involved with?"

Miranda nodded. She turned and looked at Dessie. "Please don't say anything to anyone. I'm not sure, but I think he and Jules are getting…close."

"Close?" Dessie squealed. "You mean they're hot for each other?" She slapped her forehead. "Of course! Why didn't I think of that before? How perfect. I don't like him much, but that's my problem."

Miranda sighed. "I'm not sure they're that perfect for each other. Rory has this gentle, caring side and is easily hurt. Jules can be so rough sometimes."

"Maybe he'll soften her?" Dessie suggested. "I hope he does. It might convince her to see me and hear my side of the story."

Miranda looked doubtful. "I wouldn't hold my breath if

I were you. But…" She paused. "You might have a chance if you worked on Rory."

Dessie frowned. "How do you mean?"

Miranda smiled. "Try to get him on your side. Be sweet to him. Then he'll get Jules to change her mind."

Dessie laughed. "That's a dirty trick, but I like it. I'll work out a way to butter Rory up. I think I know where to begin already…"

"Oh, God," Miranda mumbled. "What have I started?"

* * *

She was back. Driving home, Rory couldn't stop thinking about Dessie standing there in the kitchen, looking as if butter wouldn't melt. The brazen hussy, who had been instrumental in breaking up Jules and Harry's marriage and then acted like a wronged woman and left town in a huff, giving them all the finger. She hadn't sent as much as a postcard to her sisters during her ten-year absence. Jules had been devastated, losing both a sister and a husband. The marriage had been a sham from then on, until Harry's sudden death seven years later. Jules had struggled on, bringing up her son and running the house and farm as best she could. And now, when things were finally turning around, the business of breeding top-class event horses taking off, Tony doing well at school, and Jules finding happiness at last, here she was. He couldn't get over the sight of Dessie, standing there, all grown up and stunning, with her glossy black hair, doe eyes and endless legs. His hands shook as he tried to keep them steady on the wheel.

A thought struck him as he drove past the gates of Knocknagow House. Did Jules know? Maybe he should break the news to her before anyone else did. He stopped the jeep and backed up, turning in through the gates as fast as he could. He drove around the back of the big house and saw the lights in the kitchen. She was still up. He pulled up and jumped down from the jeep as Jules opened the back door and peered out, accompanied by a motley crew of assorted dogs barking furiously.

"Rory? What's up?" she asked. "Has something happened?"

"Yes." He took her arm. "I'll tell you when we're inside. You need to sit down when you hear this."

"Hear what?" Jules demanded when she was finally sitting down on one of the chairs at the kitchen table. "Has someone died?"

"No. But this might still come as a shock." He put his hand on her shoulder. "Jules, Dessie's back."

She looked at him blankly. "And?"

"You knew."

"Of course I bloody knew," she snapped. "Dessie called me herself last night. How did you find out?"

Rory pulled up a chair and sat down. "I called in to Miranda just now, and there she was, bold as brass, having dinner."

Jules shrugged. "Why shouldn't she? They were always close. Dessie didn't do anything to Miranda, after all."

"I know. But what's she doing here? Why did she come back?"

"Killybeg. It's going to be sold. She's working for some auctioneers in London who're handling the sale of the contents. It appears our little Dessie has a degree from Trinity and is now working for this London firm. Weird, huh?"

"Incredible. Never thought she had it in her." Rory studied Jules. "Are you okay?"

"I'm fine. Hearing Dessie's voice was a shock, I have to admit. I haven't thought much about her for a long time. The whole thing just kind of faded away." Jules rose from the chair. "How about something to eat? I haven't had a chance to have dinner. I just came in from feeding the horses and clipping Sam. I'm riding him in the opening meet on Monday."

"I haven't had dinner yet either. Do you want to go out somewhere?"

Jules laughed and ran her hand through her short blonde hair. "I look a mess. And I didn't have time to cook. But fear not, I have some of Miranda's Moroccan lamb stew in the freezer. I'll just chuck that in the oven for twenty minutes and make rice."

Rory relaxed. "Sounds great." He eyed her dishevelled appearance. "I'll make the rice if you want to, uh, freshen up."

Jules looked down at her torn jeans and stained sweatshirt and laughed. "I'll run upstairs and have a bit of a wash. I can tell that the stable lad look isn't terribly seductive."

Rory smiled and shook his head. "You're seductive no matter how you look."

"Liar." Jules laughed and ran upstairs.

Rory smiled to himself as he put water to boil for the rice. Jules was lovely when she was in a good mood. Their relationship was growing into something wonderful and comforting. After all the years of turmoil and conflict with his mother, he was finally in a good place. Jules was an interesting woman, full of fun but with depths he had never known until they started dating. They shared so many things: a love of nature and animals, and a passion for horses. Jules could be moody and difficult at times, quick to anger and too ready to jump to conclusions. Perhaps a little judgemental too, but who was perfect? There were no dramas or complications in their relationship. Maybe it was a little short on passion, but at forty-two he had stopped yearning for that kind of thing. This warm friendship was bound to turn into something deeper with time. If only the younger sister didn't stir up trouble again. She was a born rebel, and, at nineteen, had been a scandal waiting to happen. Yes, he had lusted after her, just like all the men in town, young or old. She had a bold face and still did. That look in her eyes that challenged you, dared you to…

"Ta-da!" Jules' voice jolted him back to the present. He looked up to find her standing in the door, dressed in a tight black top and skinny jeans. Her hair gleamed, her face was freshly made up, and she had even put on a pair of gold hoop earrings.

"Wow," he said, laughing. "That's some transformation!"

Jules sashayed into the kitchen. "Yeah, and it only took me fifteen minutes." She did a twirl. "Not bad for a tough old bird, eh?"

He put his arm around her. "Old? At thirty-five? You're still a spring chicken, sweetheart. I'm the oldie around here."

She patted his chest. "You're in your prime. Men never grow old. Especially not hunks like you. Come on, let's eat before I starve to death." She winked. "And then, who knows?"

He felt a fleeting dart of excitement, but then the image of Dessie's long legs popped into his mind. Confused, he pushed the thoughts away and went to help Jules serve supper. The delicious smell of the lamb stew made his stomach rumble. He smiled at Jules and sat down at the table. Food, wine, and then…would their friendship turn into something else?

* * *

They started work the following day, despite it being Sunday. Marcus had booked a horse for the opening meet of the Cloughmichael Foxhounds on the Monday, so he wanted to get a head start on the cataloguing. Dessie had given in despite her feelings about hunting. She had to keep Marcus sweet. Her job was more important than animal rights. She was looking forward to getting stuck into the indexing, and she couldn't wait to prove to him she was up to the task.

Armed with a notebook, pens, and her iPad, she entered the house. Marcus was already walking through the downstairs rooms taking photographs with what looked like an expensive camera. She caught up with him in the drawing room, where he was standing in front of an occasional table crammed with ornaments.

He turned around as she entered. "Morning. I'm just having a look around and trying to decide in which order to list the items. But then I decided, as this is such a mishmash kind of house, to just list stuff as we go along. It'll make the auction more interesting." He pointed at a watercolour on the wall. "What do you make of this one? Do you have a clue about who the artist might have been?"

Dessie went to his side and peered at the picture. She studied it for a few minutes. "I think it's by Robert Stopford. A scene depicting the Queen's Old Castle department store in Cork city." She pointed at the lower right-hand corner of the painting. "It's signed here, with the date, 1848. One of the Hourigan ancestors managed this store in the late nineteenth century, I believe. I think this is quite a unique picture. I'd say it's worth about fifteen hundred euros, maybe more."

Marcus looked impressed. "Oh, really? Okay. Let's make this lot number one, then. Should kick-start the auction nicely." He aimed his camera at the picture and took a few shots.

"Nice camera," she remarked.

"Yes. It's a Canon EOS 700 D. It's fabulous for this kind of work." He looked at Dessie with approval. "Great beginning. I'm glad the old pater picked you to assist. You're terrific."

"Thank you." Dessie wrote the details into her notebook.

"You take compliments with ease," he remarked.

She glanced at him. "I didn't take that as a compliment.

It's a fact. I *am* terrific. This is an important assignment for me, and I aim to do my job professionally and correctly."

He hung his head. "I stand corrected. No compliments during working hours."

She nodded and turned the page on her notepad. "Next?"

"You choose."

"What about that bookcase?" Dessie nodded at the opposite wall.

Marcus followed her gaze. "Yes. Fine piece. Gothic style. George IV."

"Yes, except the base is William IV," Dessie cut in. "Kind of symbolic, don't you think? I mean the older brother on top of the younger brother. I'd love to have a Victorian piece next."

Marcus shot Dessie a look of surprise mingled with respect. "You know your history."

Dessie nodded. "Of course. I don't think I would have gotten a first at Trinity if I didn't."

"A first? Well done! I didn't reach such heights at university."

Dessie shrugged with false modesty. "All because I had an amazing tutor."

He smirked. "I see."

She glared at him. "It was a woman. She was sixty-two. Just in case you thought something else."

He raised his hands. "Absolutely not. What would that 'something else' be anyway?"

"Oh, shut up. Let's keep going. You want to get a head start so you can get up on that horse and chase a defenceless little animal tomorrow."

He didn't rise to her bait but mumbled, "Indeed," and moved along the wall to a series of watercolours of hunting scenes. He looked at them for a while then picked up his camera and took a few shots. "What do you make of these?" he said over his shoulder. "Henry Thomas Alken? Not quite Stubbs, but rather nice."

Dessie moved to his side and looked at the pictures. "Yes. I agree with all of that." She wrote it down in her notebook. "Lot number three, then?"

"Yes, okay. Value?"

Dessie thought for a moment. "Haven't a clue. Between three and five hundred each?"

"Sounds good."

They continued on for several hours, until Marcus looked at his watch and announced it was lunchtime. "Time for a break, don't you think?"

Dessie looked up from her notes. "Lunchtime already? Gosh, I got so caught up with it all, I forgot the time." She pointed at two large porcelain figures on a desk. "We forgot to take down the details of those. I looked at them earlier. They're Meissen. Should fetch a couple of thousand at least. Take the picture, and then I'll put them as lot fifty-two. Two thousand euros."

"Okay." Marcus took the picture, and then lowered the camera. "I just realised that there must be twenty thousand euros worth of stuff in this room alone. We haven't even done half of it."

"I know."

"There's still the silver in the dining room. And the paintings in the library. By the time we've finished, I'm sure we'll have clocked up close to a million, maybe more."

Dessie nodded. "You're right. I never thought of it like that."

He shook his head in disbelief. "And all of this has been sitting here unsecured for decades, with only a series of housekeepers to keep an eye on it? It's a miracle the house wasn't ransacked years ago."

"That's true. But…" Dessie stopped. "This might sound unbelievable."

"Go on."

"Well, first of all, very few people would know about the

things here, or believe there was much worth stealing. The house has been hidden away in the grounds for so long that people have forgotten about it. And the façade is dilapidated and wrecked-looking. You'd never guess that the interior is anything special."

Marcus nodded. "I suppose. But still...why wouldn't the occasional crook sneak in and have a look around?"

"Because of the old stories."

"What old stories?"

"That the house is haunted."

Marcus looked incredulous. "What? You're having me on. If there were ghosts, wouldn't we have felt it?" He made a wide gesture at the French windows, where the late autumn sun streamed in, bathing the room in a golden light. "This room has a restful vibe. Nostalgic, but kind of warm and loving."

Dessie nodded. "Yes. Down here there are no ghosts. But you haven't been upstairs yet, in *that* room..." She fought to keep a straight face as she watched Marcus' expression change. She *was* having him on, but there was a grain of truth in what she said. The room she thought was the nursery had felt decidedly spooky ten years earlier. Those dolls staring at her, the rocking horse frozen in motion, and the half-open wardrobe...

"What room?" he snapped. "Stop playing games. I thought you said you'd be professional."

"Just a little warning. Thought you should be prepared," Dessie said in a cool voice and closed her notebook. "Time for lunch, as you said. I think we've done enough for today, actually. I promised Audrey I'd walk up the mountains with her this afternoon anyway. It's a shame to be indoors when the sun is shining. But of course, you can carry on alone if you wish."

He nodded and put his camera in its case. "Okay. Fine with me. Let's close shop for today. Maybe we could have lunch at that little pub nearby? Looks very quaint."

"No thank you. I made sandwiches for Audrey and me to take on our walk. Maybe you'd care to join us?"

"On the walk? Or just for lunch?"

"Both, if you like. It's quite a steep climb to where we're going. You might not be fit enough for that."

"Is this a dare?"

Dessie shrugged. "Whatever you want to call it. You're welcome to join us."

"Thanks, but not this time. I'll have lunch at the pub and come back here to take some more photos."

"Okay. Just make sure not to go upstairs on your own."

"Now, that I take as a dare."

Dessie smirked. "Could be. Only one way to find out."

Marcus winked. "I'll keep you posted."

CHAPTER 8

As she was not going to the opening meet of the fox hunting season, Dessie looked forward to a quiet day. She could hear Marcus and Audrey chatting in the kitchen, talking about hunting, no doubt. Dessie turned her pillow to the cool side and snuggled under the duvet, drifting back to sleep, only to be startled by her phone ringing on the bedside table. She grunted and picked it up.

"Mmm?"

It was Miranda. "Morning, pet. Are you going to the opening meet?"

"No," Dessie mumbled. "I'm still in bed. Thought I'd sleep in."

"I think you should go. It's a beautiful day. It would also be a great opportunity to show everyone you're back. The whole town goes to the opening meet."

Dessie sat up. "That's a very good reason *not* to go."

"Well, yes. I know it'll be hard for you, but this way you'd get it over with in one go. And Rory will be there. You could chat him up in the pub when the hunt has moved off."

Dessie made a face. "Oh, shit, no. Do I have to? I thought he'd be hunting."

"His horse is lame. But he'll be following on foot. Come on, Dessie. It mightn't be so bad. You can't hide in the gatehouse forever."

"Are you going?"

"No, I can't. I have a huge amount of work to do on the farm. But Audrey's going. She's reporting on the event for the paper. I already spoke to her. She'll give you a lift in her car, she said."

Dessie rolled her eyes. Typical. Miranda, the control freak. A heart of pure gold, but with an irritating habit of organising everyone's life. "All right, then," she snapped. "I'll go. But it'll be your fault if the mob lynches me."

"Don't be melodramatic. You'll be fine. They have all forgotten about it and moved on. They probably won't even notice you."

"Yeah, right. But whatever. I'll go. As you said, I might as well bite the bullet and show my face."

"Good girl. Call me later and let me know how it went."

"If I'm still alive."

* * *

She knew within minutes of walking down the main street, crammed with horse boxes, horses, and riders in full hunting dress, that nobody had forgotten her. Heads turned and eyebrows were raised as she walked down the street beside Audrey and Dan, the newspaper photographer. Dessie stuck out her chin and walked on, pretending she didn't see the sideways glances or hear the whispers and mutterings.

"Look at her. Bold as brass," someone said behind her.

Dessie glanced at the woman over her shoulder. "Hello, Maura. Yes, I'm back. Thanks for the welcome. Lovely day, isn't it?"

The woman turned a deep shade of pink and turned away without answering.

"What was that all about?" Audrey asked. "Why are people staring at you and whispering?"

Dessie shrugged. "They're reliving the past. I left ten years ago under a bit of a cloud. They all thought I had done something I didn't do, but they have no idea what I actually did, which was nearly as bad."

Audrey and Dan stopped and stared at Dessie.

"I have a feeling that's all you're going to say." Audrey sighed. "But it sounds like a hell of a story." She nudged Dan in the ribs. "How about you? You're from around here. You must know what Dessie did—or didn't."

He shrugged. "Nah, no idea. My mum didn't like gossip, so I never got to hear the juicy stories. Anyway, I was in Dublin doing journalism at UCD at the time."

"Shit," Audrey muttered. "That means I have to ask the locals, and they'll tell me their side, which is never the truth. I'll just have to forget it until Dessie agrees to tell me."

"I might if I'm drunk." Dessie laughed.

Audrey's eyes narrowed. "Hmm...that could be arranged."

Dessie was about to reply when she spotted Jules riding down the street on a big chestnut horse. Without thinking, Dessie ran to greet her, grabbing the reins. "Hi, Jules. What a beautiful day. And what a fabulous horse. Is this Sam?"

"Yes." Jules pulled the horse up and looked down at Dessie. "What are you doing here? I thought you were against fox hunting and everything to do with it."

"Oh, I am. I hate any kind of blood sport. But I thought it was a good opportunity to piss everyone off by showing up."

"Mission accomplished, then." Without another word, Jules wheeled her horse around and trotted off in the opposite direction.

Dessie stared at Jules' departing figure. She looked strong and happy despite her sniping. Was this due to her budding love affair with Rory? In that case, making friends with him might be the best way to soften Jules. She looked around for him in the crowd, but she couldn't see him anywhere.

Maybe he was late? She did see Marcus, however, looking like something out of *Horse & Hound* magazine on a huge bay horse with a plaited mane. She couldn't help noticing his muscular thighs in the tight white breeches, and the set of his broad shoulders in the black hunting jacket. The white stock tied in a bow secured with a gold pin added to his rakish appearance. There was a man made for fox hunting.

He trotted his horse up to Dessie and raised his hunting cap. "Morning ma'am. Fancy seeing you here, considering how you feel about hunting."

"I came to see you," she replied with a sweet smile. "I wanted to see you in full hunting regalia. You look good enough to eat. Is that horse big enough for you?"

He shot her a dazzling smile. "He's rather big, but I've been assured he can handle those famous Irish banks. All I have to do is hang on, pray, and hope for the best."

"Modest too," Dessie purred. "Well, good luck, Marcus. Have a lovely day."

"The same to you, m'dear." He put two fingers to his cap in a mock salute and trotted the horse to join the rest of the hunt farther down the street.

The hounds were released from their trailer, and Dessie watched the stream of black-and-tan dogs trotting down the ramp. So sleek and glossy. Beautiful animals, despite being trained to kill. The pack gathered around the horse of the whipper-in waiting for the off. The huntsman blew his horn, and horses and riders moved down the street, the clatter of hundreds of hooves echoing through the town. Despite her aversion to fox hunting, Dessie had to admit the sight of red coats, hounds, and horses against the backdrop of the trees in blazing colours was beautiful in its timeless way.

When the horses and riders had disappeared to the first covert, most of the onlookers made their way to the pub for a drink before either going home, or setting off to follow the hunt on foot. Dessie caught sight of Rory heading into

Mulligan's, which she knew was his local. Great place for a quiet chat. She gathered up what little courage she possessed and entered the pub, scanning the dim interior for Rory's dark head and broad shoulders. She found him standing by the bar, trying to catch the attention of the bartender.

She sidled up to him, clearing her throat. "Hi, Rory," she shouted over the din of many voices. "Not riding today?"

He turned, looking startled. "Hi. No, my horse is lame. I'm following on foot later."

"I just saw Jules on a fabulous chestnut."

He nodded. "Yes. That's Sam, her baby. One of the best hunters around here." He waved at the barman. "Hey, Paddy," he yelled. "When you have a chance, pull us a pint, willya?"

Paddy focused his eyes on Rory. "Sure thing, Rory. Howerya, Dessie? Great to see you back. What'll you have?"

"A glass of Harp, please," she replied. "And Rory's pint's on me."

"No," Rory protested. "I'll get your beer."

"Please. Let me get this one," Dessie pleaded. "Just as a peace offering."

Rory looked puzzled. "Peace offering? I don't think we need that. We never had a fight or anything, did we?"

Dessie shrugged. "Not really, but we weren't exactly bosom buddies, now, were we?"

"I suppose." He studied her for a moment. "You look so different."

She met his gaze. "In what way?"

He gestured at her pink sneakers, skinny jeans, and green suede jacket. "Sleek. Sophisticated. Glamorous and bloody confident. Far from the brazen little hussy who left all that disaster in her wake."

She cocked her head and smiled, just to show her dimples. "Should I take that as a compliment?"

Their drinks arrived, saving Rory from replying. "Do you want to stay here at the bar, or sit down somewhere?" he asked.

Dessie scanned the packed pub. "Where? I don't see a square millimetre to sit on. Let's stay here. In any case, if we were to sit down in a quiet corner, people might start talking and saying I'm stealing my sister's man all over again."

Rory's face flushed. "I don't know what you mean. Jules and I are just friends."

"Methinks the gentleman protests too much," Dessie teased. "Why hide it? If you and Jules are getting…close, why don't you two show it to the world? Nervous about what people might think? Or…are you still scared of your mammy?"

He glared at her. "Why don't you mind your own business?"

She bristled. "Why didn't you and your mammy mind yours all those years ago? Have you ever stopped to think that it might all have been lies?"

"Oh, I did. I thought a lot about it at the time. But the way you flounced out of here and just disappeared had guilt written all over it. If you had stayed, you might have turned the tide around."

Dessie drained her glass and slid from the bar stool. "Are you kidding? A nineteen-year-old girl against the whole town? I had to leave. I couldn't take the hostility, the whispers, the dirty looks, and most of all, Jules and her anger. Harry tried to tell her what really happened. But she wanted to believe he was guilty, so she refused to listen." Dessie drew breath and threw a ten euro bill on the counter. "That should cover the drinks, plus a tip."

Rory put his hand on her arm. "Don't go off in a huff, Dessie. I didn't mean—what you thought I meant. I've been thinking about all of this since the other day when we met again at Miranda's. Can we…?" He stopped and looked at the crowd over his shoulder. "I'd like to talk to you, but it's difficult in this place. Too noisy. I don't want to have to shout."

"Don't you want to follow the hunt?"

"Yes." He looked at his watch. "They should be at the second covert by now. They usually draw a blank at the first one."

Dessie nodded. "Yes, and they have to jump that big bank at the back field, and then there's the hedge and the stream."

"You know the country well, considering you hate hunting."

"I used to go out with the pony club before I was old enough to know better."

"I remember. You were a big chicken too. Always squealing and screaming at every fence."

Dessie laughed. "You know me too well, Rory Quirke."

His eyes softened. "Them were the days, Dessie, weren't they?"

"Before we lost our innocence."

"Will you follow the hunt with me?"

Dessie raised an eyebrow. "You and me in your jeep? Are you mad? Just imagine the gossip afterwards. Not to mention that Jules will have a fit. In any case, I don't want to watch a fox being chased by a pack of bloodthirsty hounds. I'm going for a walk up the hills, and then I'm going back with Audrey and Dan. I have some work to do on the cataloguing too. I have to transfer my notes to the file on my laptop and download the photos Marcus took yesterday."

He sighed and nodded. "Okay. You're right. I'll be off in a minute too. Have a nice walk, Dessie."

"Thanks." She looked at him for a moment, hesitating. It had gone well, but the opportunity to have a proper talk had slipped away. "See you soon, I hope," she said, looking into his eyes.

"I'd like that. Bye, Dessie. Thanks for the pint. Next one's on me."

"I'll hold you to that," she shouted over her shoulder as she walked out of the pub, no longer caring if anyone heard. Let them talk. As long as Jules didn't hear them.

* * *

They returned to the big house the following day. Marcus, although tired after many hours in the saddle during a challenging hunt, was eager to get back to work. Dessie didn't complain. The house promised to be a treasure trove of antiques and artefacts that would put the forthcoming auction at the top of the news stories in the media for days. It could be a huge coup for Smythe's.

They slowly made their way through the rest of the items in the drawing room, discovering exquisite items of great value among more mundane things that would fetch a good price simply because of their age.

As eleven o'clock approached, Marcus put down his camera. "How about a coffee break? I feel I need to rest my eyes for a bit."

Dessie nodded and closed her notebook. "Yes, me too. And we've nearly finished this room. Let's have some coffee and then do the rest when we come back. Audrey said she put the coffee maker and biscuits in the kitchen downstairs, so we can have it there. That way we can look around the basement on our way."

Marcus laughed. "You're really hooked, aren't you?"

Dessie smiled. "Yes, I suppose I am. Aren't you?"

He nodded. "It's an interesting house. But to you, it must mean a lot more. Part of your heritage in a way."

Dessie led the way down the winding staircase from the hall. "The house has always been sitting here behind the walls, waiting for me," she said, her voice echoing in the dark space. She turned. "Could you hit that switch on the wall? I can't see a thing."

"Yes, sorry." Marcus flicked a switch, and the staircase was illuminated in an eerie light. "This looks older than the rest of the house," he remarked.

Dessie touched the stones of the curved wall as she

carefully made her way down the stairs. "There was an old castle here, and the house was built on what was left of the foundations. There could have been a dungeon here for all we know. But there isn't much left of that, just these walls and the floor in the wine cellar."

They arrived at the bottom of the stairs, where a door led to a large country kitchen with two stoves, a huge, worn pine table, and oak cupboards revealing an array of copper cookware, earthenware pots, china mixing bowls and other paraphernalia. Bright sunlight shone through the windows set high on the far wall, making square patterns on the floor tiles. The room smelled of damp and turf, with a slight whiff of onions and gravy.

Marcus looked around. "Fantastic. You can really imagine the kitchen staff preparing feasts for the gentry down here."

"I can still smell the stews they must have cooked here." Dessie walked to the espresso machine and rummaged through a collection of coffee pods in a plastic box. "What kind of coffee do you want? Espresso?"

"If there's a longer one, I'll have that."

Dessie picked up a purple pod. "This one says Vivalto Lungo. I've had it before. It's good."

Marcus nodded. "Make one for me, please." He walked across the floor into another, smaller room and peered in. "What's this? The pantry?"

Dessie filled the container at the back of the espresso maker with water. "I think it was the butler's room, where he did the bookkeeping or something."

"It's empty, except for a trunk. I wonder what's in it."

"Why don't you have a look?" Dessie suggested while she made the coffee.

"Coffee first." Marcus took the cup Dessie handed him.

"Yes, me too." Dessie made herself a cup of cappuccino. "I need coffee at eleven. My brain doesn't work without it."

Marcus' blue eyes smiled at her over the rim of his cup. "I

think we're kindred spirits. Coffee-kindred, anyway. Is this a sign?"

"Of what?" Dessie asked airily.

He shrugged and put his cup on the counter. "Compatibility?"

"I think you'd need a lot more proof than just coffee."

Marcus winked. "It's a start. I mean, imagine if you said you never drink coffee and just had to have a cup of dandelion tea at twelve? I couldn't bond with someone like that."

Dessie looked away from his twinkling eyes. "Who says we need to bond? We just need to work well together." She rinsed the cups under the tap. "Come on, let's look at what's in the trunk. Maybe some buried treasure?"

"Or a collection of dirty books from the Victorian era?" Marcus suggested, still with that annoying grin. Was he having fun making her uncomfortable?

"We'll soon know." Dessie marched across the tiles into the small room to where a large leather chest sat in the middle of the dusty floor. It had stickers from hotels and cruise ships, and the leather straps were torn off. A bright red silk ribbon stuck out from the slightly open lid.

"Looks like it wasn't unpacked," Marcus quipped.

Dessie tried to lift the lid. "It's stuck."

"Here, let me." Marcus yanked at the lid with both hands and it slowly opened with a creaky sound that startled them both.

Dessie twisted her head away. "What's in it? I'm afraid to look."

Marcus looked into the trunk and gasped.

CHAPTER 9

"What is it?" Dessie whispered. "A body?"

"No. Look for yourself. Amazing."

Dessie turned back and looked into the trunk, steeling herself for something shocking. But all she could see was an array of silk dresses, some dusty and torn, some carefully wrapped in tissue paper, tiny silk purses, ribbons, gloves, and even shoes. She pulled out the dress on the top, a long, slinky silk gown covered in roses and butterflies. "Oh, how beautiful." She held it up to the light. "Pity it's so torn." She shook out the dress and sneezed. "Sorry, the dust…"

Marcus waved his hand in the air. "I know. It's covered in it." He peered into the trunk and touched the next dress, blue silk and sequins visible through layers of tissue paper. "This one is in better shape," he said as he pulled it out. The tissue paper floated to the floor in a soft whisper. "It's gorgeous."

Dessie's breath caught in her throat. "It's exquisite." She touched the diamanté beads around the neckline. "Look at the work on this one. Must be some kind of designer dress of the era. Nineteen thirty or so, would you say?"

Marcus turned the dress this way and that. "Yes. Early thirties. Paris. Worth, or…Schiaparelli?" He paused for a moment. "Or Balenciaga, perhaps. Is there a label?"

Dessie took the dress and looked inside the neckline. "Yes. Very faded. I can see a H and an E…"

"Heim," Marcus said. "Jacques Heim. Very fashionable in the thirties. He started his couture house in 1930 in Paris."

"You know a lot about vintage fashion."

Marcus smiled. "I had to bone up on this period when we did that castle in Scotland. There was a big collection of vintage clothes there."

Dessie put the dress on the desk and pulled out another gown in plain red silk with a white collar. "I think this is a tea gown. Also lovely."

"But who wore them? I had no idea this kind of dress would have been the thing in an Irish country house in the thirties."

"The Hourigans were very fashionable," Dessie replied, delving into the trunk once more. "They threw a lot of parties and balls, and they often travelled to Dublin for big functions there. These dresses must have belonged to Conchita, who was married to Tom Hourigan. A beautiful Spanish woman. She lived here until 1936, when she left to fight in the Spanish Civil War. She never returned. Believed to have been killed in a bomb explosion. So sad. I think there are photos of her in one of those dusty family albums we never bothered to look at."

Marcus didn't reply. He was busy unwrapping yet another dress, this one of ivory silk with green trim and belt. "Looks like she spent a lot of money on clothes before she became a freedom fighter."

"She might have run away from her husband. He was a lot older than her and rumoured to be temperamental and mean when he got drunk."

"Yes, maybe," Marcus mumbled with an odd look in his eyes. He held the dress up against Dessie. "You'd look lovely in something like this."

She backed away. "Not really my style."

"Perhaps not, but I have an idea."

"I'm not dressing up in these old clothes," Dessie protested, suddenly aware they were all alone in the big house.

"Please, don't get all prissy. I wasn't going to suggest anything kinky. I was thinking…a vintage fashion shoot. You and Audrey could model these and pose in the drawing room and dining room. Dreamy, nostalgic shots. Maybe even in the garden? It could be great publicity for the auction."

"I'm not into modelling. Audrey is the editor-in-chief of a newspaper. She might not want to—"

"Ah, come on," Marcus pleaded. "It's not as if I suggested bikini shots. It's just to market the house and its contents, and to make it into something really unique. Besides, how do you know what Audrey will say? She might love the idea. The dresses are gorgeous. Wouldn't any woman love to wear them, if just for an hour or two?"

Dessie's gaze drifted to the pile of silk on the table. "They're musty and smell of mould."

"We'll hang them outside for a bit. I'm sure a little fresh air will help. I have a feeling they were only worn a couple of times anyway, so they would have been quite clean when they were put away."

Dessie softened. He was right. The dresses were lovely and she was dying to try them on, float around the drawing room, and pretend she was a rich lady, like those girls in *Downton Abbey*, each episode of which she had watched at least three times. That era was still in vogue after the TV series. She gently lifted the ivory dress and packed it back into the tissue paper. "Okay, I see what you mean. I think it could be a good idea. Let's talk to Audrey at dinner tonight and see if she'll agree. Otherwise, I'll do it on my own."

Marcus smiled. "That's the spirit! I was thinking you could pose against a backdrop of some of the paintings or the most valuable pieces of furniture. Like that seventeenth-century ormolu clock on the period mantelpiece in the library."

Dessie nodded. "Yes. Something like that." She was

suddenly gripped by a wave of excitement. This would be a whole new kind of publicity. And her name would be in the catalogue for all to see. She might even be promoted. She wrapped the dresses and put them back in the trunk. They'd look at the rest of the contents later. "Let's go and find that album," she suggested. "Maybe Conchita is in one of the photos. Then we could do a re-enactment and match two similar pictures."

Marcus nodded. "Brilliant idea. You're good at this marketing stuff. And here I was, thinking you were just a pretty face."

"Ha," Dessie snorted and walked out of the room. "You ain't seen nothing yet."

They found the albums in the morning room, next to the dining room, on a table with piles of books and ledgers. Dessie pulled out the leather-bound book and opened it, looking through pictures of men in morning suit, women in riding clothes standing stiffly beside their horses held by grooms, children in lace dresses on the knees of their nannies, and people in evening dress in drawing rooms stuffed with furniture and potted plants.

She flicked the pages. "What artificial lives they led. Always on show, always accompanied by servants. Nobody's smiling." She scanned the pages and suddenly squealed. "Here she is! Look!" She passed the open album to Marcus. "See that black-haired woman standing by the window? That has to be Conchita, and she's wearing the ivory dress. God, she's beautiful."

Marcus peered at the photo. "Fabulous woman. I can tell she was sexy even from this photo. Such smouldering eyes…" He sighed. "I think I'm in love. I wish there were a time machine I could get into."

"Yes, she was really something," Dessie agreed. "Turn the page, maybe there are more photos of her."

Marcus turned the pages. "Here's one with her in riding

clothes. She's wearing jodhpurs. I bet that was kind of avant-garde in those days."

Dessie looked at the photo. Conchita was sitting on a big black horse, laughing into the camera. "She looks like she's having fun being daring. It says June 1936 underneath. Must have been just before she left. What a shame she died like that."

"Sad." Marcus closed the album. His eyes focused on Dessie. "Do you think you can recreate that spirit? I have a feeling there's hot fire behind that cool, professional exterior."

Dessie felt her face flush, not because of his words, but the look in his eyes. "Whatever is under my surface is none of your business," she snapped. "I thought we agreed on a professional relationship at all times."

Her words had the desired effect. He closed the album. "I know. I keep forgetting. My apologies."

"Accepted."

Marcus took a deep breath and rubbed his hands together. "Okay, let's get back to work. We have to finish this room today and get started on the dining room. Otherwise, we'll never finish."

Dessie put the album back. "Okay. We can start with this pile of stuff. Do you think anyone wants to buy the album?"

"No. The owner wants to keep any family photos and albums. He'll be here himself just before the auction."

Dessie's stomach flipped. "He's coming here? I had no idea."

"Yes." Marcus walked to the far end of the room. "He wants to attend the auction. I'm looking forward to meeting him, aren't you?"

"Of course," Dessie said, her voice coming out in a hoarse whisper. "Should be...interesting."

* * *

Audrey would have none of the modelling. "Forget it," she snapped when Marcus asked her at dinner. "I hate having my photograph taken. I don't even do selfies."

"Why?" Marcus asked, staring at her. "You look fantastic."

"That won't make me change my mind." Audrey got up, taking her plate to the dishwasher. "Thanks for dinner, Marcus. It was delicious. Sorry, but I have to go. Some stuff to do before we put the paper to bed for tomorrow's issue." She was about to walk out of the room but stopped and twirled around at the door. "You know who'd be perfect with Dessie in those photos? Miranda. She has that slender, old-fashioned look. I can see the two of you floating around in those misty, dreamy photos." She kissed her fingers. "Divine."

"Yes, but—" Marcus started.

"Think about it. I'd get Dan to take the shots. He's very good and very cheap. Bye for now." She closed the door behind her.

Marcus stared at Dessie. "What's eating her?"

Dessie shrugged and gathered up the plates. "What's eating anyone? Everyone has some kind of stuff bothering them under the glossy surface."

Marcus took a swing of wine. "Really? What's bothering you, then?"

"Let's not go there, okay?" Dessie snapped. "What about you? There has to be more to you than that British stiff-upper-lip-Hugh-Grant look."

"Nothing much." Marcus got up and helped Dessie with the plates. "Could you contact your sister and ask her about the shoot?"

"I will. Not sure she'll agree, but you never know."

"Tell me when you've talked to her." Marcus slammed the dishwasher shut. "Got to go. Stuff to do. See you tomorrow." He walked stiffly out of the kitchen.

"What's up with them?" Dessie asked Cat, who had just wandered in from the utility room.

Cat looked at her with golden eyes and meowed.

"Don't know either, huh?" Dessie poured milk in a saucer and put it on the floor. She jumped as the door flew open and Marcus came back into the kitchen. "What's up?" she asked him. "You look as if you've seen a ghost."

Marcus ran his hand through his hair, his face white. "You could say that. The ghost of a dead woman who's come back to cause trouble."

Dessie's jaw dropped. "Who...?"

"Conchita."

"What on earth are you going on about?" Dessie demanded. "Stop talking in riddles."

Marcus sank down on a chair. "Sorry. I just had a huge shock. My father called. It appears there's a dispute about ownership of Killybeg."

Dessie's head swam. "Ownership? But Richard Hourigan is the owner, isn't he? He was the sole heir to his father's estate."

Marcus nodded. "So he says. But now it seems that Conchita and Tom Hourigan weren't properly married."

"Says who?"

"The descendant of Tom Hourigan's cousin."

"But, but…," Dessie stammered, "is this possible?"

Marcus nodded. "Extremely possible, my father says. He just called me to tell me. There's going to be a legal dispute that could take years."

"Jesus." Dessie flopped down on the chair beside Marcus. "What do we do now?"

"Nothing," he sighed. "We can't go ahead with the auction until this is resolved. Richard Hourigan has no right to sell as much as a postage stamp, until this is cleared up. We might even be in breach of the law just going into the house." He slammed his fist on the table. "Fuck! And this was going to be one of the best auctions ever."

"Oh God," Dessie whispered. "What a disaster." She stared at Marcus. "Who is this distant cousin? And why has he—or she—come forward now?"

"It's a she. Some woman in Dublin. There was a piece about the forthcoming auction in The Irish Times last week. Apparently, she looked up her family tree and started digging. That's all I know."

"So what do we do?" Dessie asked.

"Father is looking into the issue. He said we might continue with the cataloguing if we can find out if it's legal. The solicitor is going to let us know. The consensus is that it would be useful to have a catalogue of the contents of the house. But there might be no auction at the end of it."

"What about Richard Hourigan? What can he do?"

Marcus shrugged. "He could try to find the marriage licence. There is no record of Tom Hourigan having married Conchita in this country."

"Maybe they were married in Spain?" Dessie suggested. "The records could have been destroyed during the civil war."

Marcus shrugged. "In that case, he doesn't have a hope in hell."

Something suddenly struck Dessie. "Maybe…" she started, "if we search…" She looked at Marcus and saw he was thinking the same thing.

He shot up from his chair. "You're right! The marriage certificate could very well be somewhere in the house."

"Let's go and look tomorrow," Dessie replied.

Marcus nodded, looking cheerful. "We must." He stopped. "Only…"

"Only what?"

"Don't tell *anyone* about this."

CHAPTER 10

Dessie was up before sunrise the next morning. Showered and dressed, she tiptoed into the kitchen as the clock on the wall struck seven. After a quick breakfast, she threw on her rain mac, stuck her feet in her wellies and hurried up the avenue toward the dark house looming on the hill. The wind blew her hair around her face and big drops of rain plopped onto her head as she ran. The path was slippery with wet leaves, and the air smelled of damp earth. She'd better get inside before the rain got heavier. She didn't have the keys, but she knew one of the basement windows would be easy to open. She'd bet it hadn't been fixed since she and Richard were there.

She was right. The faint glow in the east helped her find her way to the window. She slid her hand inside to lift the catch and managed to squeeze in without too much trouble. Inside, it was pitch-black, and Dessie stood there for a moment, breathing in the damp air. She ran her hand over the wall to find the light switch, but when she flicked it, nothing happened. Damn, the bulb must be broken. She shuffled forward, trying to remember the layout of the basement. This room must have been a storeroom for apples in the old days, judging by the lingering fruity smell. There was a long corridor that led to the kitchen, where the bulb had worked when she and Marcus were there the day before.

Dessie slowly walked forward, her hand on the cold, rough wall. She found the door to the kitchen and switched on the light. Phew. Finally. "Upwards and onwards," she said to herself and walked to the stairs, turning on lights as she went. The darkness seemed threatening down there, and she was grateful for every source of light. Arriving in the entrance hall, she was cheered by the first beams of the rising sun that penetrated the gloom. But black clouds swiftly rolled in, darkening the sky, and rain soon pelted the tall windows. At least there was still enough daylight to see. She would have no trouble finding her way.

Dessie looked down the corridor. Where to now? The study? Or the library? Where was the most likely place for old documents? She decided to start in the study, where she had spotted an old filing cabinet that must have been there since the beginning of the twentieth century. The house hadn't been lived in for over seventy years, apart from the odd visit by Tom Hourigan. It was possible that documents had been left behind.

Dessie made her way to the study on the other side of the house. The floorboards creaked and she could feel cold air on the back of her neck, like the breath of a ghost, or a whisper from the grave. She shivered and pulled her rain mac tighter, telling herself not to be silly. Reaching the closed door of the study, she was about to turn the handle when a noise made her freeze. What was that? A rustle. Someone moving inside. Had Marcus woken up before her and was already looking through the files and papers?

Dessie gently pushed the door open a crack and peeped in. Her breath caught in her throat as the figure of a man, illuminated by the old brass lamp on the desk, came into view. Marcus? No, not him she realised, but someone else, strangely familiar…

* * *

Dessie clapped her hand on her mouth. It couldn't be. Please, God, no. She peered through the crack again, looking more closely at the man standing there in the soft light of the old brass lamp. Yes, it was him. She studied him for a moment. Dressed in jeans, a blue sweater, and a pink shirt, he was still attractive despite about fifteen pounds around his middle and a thinning hairline. Her eyes drifted to an open suitcase on the floor, half-full of silver candlesticks and other items she recognised from the drawing room. He had added the two very valuable watercolours to his stash. He was stealing from the house. What a prick.

She jumped as she heard a noise behind her and turned to discover Marcus, his eyes startled. He opened his mouth to say something, but Dessie put her finger to her lips. "Shh," she whispered. "There's someone in there. Look." She stepped aside so he could see.

He looked at her through the dim light. "Who?" he mouthed.

She put her mouth to his ear. "Richard Hourigan."

"Christ." He put his eye to the gap in the open door. "Shit, he's taken some stuff from the drawing room." Marcus groped in the pocket of his Burberry. "I'm calling the cops."

But it was too late. Richard had heard them and opened the door, staring at them. "Who the hell—" His eyes focused on Dessie. "Jesus, it's you."

Dessie smiled sweetly and walked into the room, Marcus following behind her. "Yes, Richard, it's me. Hi. How are you? Long time, no see, eh?"

Richard didn't reply. He looked from Dessie to Marcus. "And this dude, who's he? Your boyfriend?"

"No," Marcus said and held out his hand. "Marcus Smythe. Of Smythe's Auctioneers."

Richard took a step back. "I see. Okay. But what's *she*... eh, doing here? Sorry, I forgot your name."

"Dessie," she said. "I know it's been a long time, but you could have remembered my name."

Richard looked only slightly uncomfortable. "I'm sorry. Of course, I remember your name. It was just the shock of seeing you here."

"Likewise. You gave me an awful fright." Her eyes drifted to the suitcase on the floor. "But there is no doubt about what you're doing here."

"What about you?" Richard snapped.

"I'm working with Marcus."

One of Richard's eyebrows shot up. "Really? You're working for Smythe's? My, you have come a long way, my little Dessie."

Sensing he was about to touch her, Dessie backed away. "Yes, I have," she said. "A long way since that summer. But let's not go there, okay? Let's talk about you taking stuff from the house. Isn't this illegal?"

Richard straightened up. "What do you mean? I have a perfect right to be here. This is my house."

Dessie's eyes narrowed. "Is it? Not for long, I hear. I see you've lifted a few of the best items. Isn't that stealing?"

Richard shrugged. "I own this property and its contents until proven otherwise, so no."

"No, you don't," Marcus cut in. "I believe all assets have been frozen. And in that case, that is stolen property."

Richard shot him a wry smile. "Really? You can't prove that."

Marcus shrugged. "Well, no. We can't prove it right now. I only know what my father just told me."

"I'll walk out of here with whatever I choose. And you can't stop me," Richard snarled.

Marcus looked at his nails in a gesture of studied nonchalance. "Very well, old man. Do what you want. You'll have to deal with the consequences when the shit hits the fan."

Dessie nodded. "It would be nice if you could make a

list of what you've taken and give me a receipt, or we'll be accused of theft. We've been cataloguing for the past week, and those items are included. For the auction. I thought you were aware of this?"

He nodded. "Yes. I asked them to do the auction. But now…"

"Yes, now what?" Dessie asked. "What's going to happen now? Do we stop the work until the issue of ownership has been resolved?"

Richard's shoulders slumped. "I don't know."

"You're in a probate situation now. Until that's over, or we find that marriage certificate, nothing can be decided." Marcus picked up his phone and took a shot of the open suitcase. "Just for the record."

"Of course," Richard mumbled.

He looked so dejected, Dessie felt a pang of pity. "I hope we find it. We came here to look for it."

Richard looked bleakly at her. "It's no use. I've been through the house and come up with nothing. It's so strange. I can't imagine that beautiful, proud woman living here like a…a…mistress or something. And then having two children out of wedlock. In 1930, that would have carried a huge stigma. It simply isn't possible."

"No," Dessie agreed. "It seems totally unbelievable. Unless she faked it."

Richard frowned and sat down on a stool by the desk. "Faked it?"

"Yes. She might have worn the wedding ring and told everyone they were married abroad. Like Spain or—"

"Yeah, that's a possibility. She was a strange woman. Very rebellious. Smoked and swore. Walked around in pants and rode like a man. Then she just left to fight in a civil war. Not your normal wife of a country squire."

"Maybe she didn't want to be married?" Marcus suggested. "She seems such a free spirit."

"We'll never know." Richard got up, switched off the light and opened the shutters. "It's still raining." He turned to face them. "Listen, this is a huge problem for me. I need the money that the auction will generate. I've spent a lot of money restoring the gatehouse. Then, when the auction is over, we'll start on the house and the other buildings. We're also building a golf course. It's a huge project that will cost millions, but it'll be a fantastic place once it's finished. We're already doing the marketing for the opening in about a year and a half." He drew breath, his eyes bleak.

"I had no idea you'd become a property tycoon," Dessie said. "I thought you were a partner in your dad's law firm."

"I was until I got in with my future father-in-law. We've been involved in some great projects in the past two years. It's a very lucrative business if you play your cards right."

"You seem to have drawn a dud hand with this one," Marcus quipped.

Richard glared at him. "Yeah. And it's my own property too. A pretty shitty situation."

"What about Courtney? What happened to her?" Dessie enquired, feeling a dart of schadenfreude. His bright, shining future hadn't panned out after all.

"Casey. We broke up after a year. I've been married twice since then. Never got it right, I guess."

"Jesus, you've had an exciting life," Dessie chortled. "And your next bride?"

"She's Irish-American. Very solid. I think she's the one, you know?"

Dessie laughed. "And doesn't she have a nice dad?"

Richard's eyes turned cold. "This is none of your business." He turned back to the window. "It stopped raining. I'm leaving now."

"On foot?" Dessie asked incredulously.

"No. My car is parked behind the house." Richard rubbed his eyes. "I've been up all night. Gone through everything. Even the bathrooms. I'm exhausted."

"Where are you staying?" Marcus asked.

"At the Bianconi."

"How did you get into the house? Do you have a key?" Marcus wanted to know.

Richard picked up the suitcase from the floor. "No. I got in through the basement. One of the windows is loose."

Dessie gave him the ghost of a smile. "That's how I got in."

He touched her shoulder. "Fond memories, eh?"

"For you, maybe," Dessie said, a bitter edge to her voice. "For me, not so fond."

He avoided her eyes. "Well, I'm off. I'll go through the front door this time. I'm going to do some more research. Tom and Conchita met in London. There are no records of them having been married there, but I'm going to have another go. Maybe the genealogist I hired has come up with something."

Marcus ran to the door and blocked his way. "Not so fast. We need that receipt. Or at least a note to say you've taken a few items. Just in case."

Richard sighed. "Okay." He fished a piece of paper from the breast pocket of his shirt. "Not much to write on, but I guess this receipt from the gas station will do."

"Doesn't matter what you write it on, as long as it has your signature," Marcus replied.

Richard went back to the desk. "I don't have a pen. Do you?"

"Never travel without one." Dessie dug in her bag and produced a biro which she handed to Richard.

He scribbled on the back of the receipt and handed it to her. "There. That should cover your ass in case of an enquiry."

Dessie didn't laugh at his attempted humour. "Thanks."

He looked at her for a moment. "I don't suppose I could ask you not to tell anyone you've seen me."

Dessie looked at Marcus. "What do you say?"

Marcus shrugged. "I'll have to tell my father. But that's the only person who needs to know. For now."

"Thanks." Richard nodded and disappeared from the room, the squeaking floorboards echoing down the corridor as he walked away.

Dessie looked at the door slowly swinging closed and wondered if it had all been a dream.

Marcus looked at her. "You and he seem to have some kind of history."

"Yeah," Dessie said. "But not something I feel like sharing. Or even remembering."

CHAPTER 11

They were silent for a long time. Marcus unbuttoned his Burberry. "Shit, what bad luck. He took the watercolours. And the Georgian candlesticks."

Dessie nodded. "I know. And the Meissen figures. He knew what'll sell easily."

Marcus sighed and sat down on a chair by the desk. "What do we do now? Keep looking?"

Dessie sat down on the chair beside him and propped her elbows on the desk, her chin in her hands. "No. No use. He said he'd looked everywhere. I'm sure he has. There has to be something we can do."

"Like what?" Marcus snapped.

"I don't know. I'm trying to think."

"Don't just sit there staring into space. If you have an idea, spit it out, for fuck's sake!" He got up and paced around the room.

"I love the way you posh guys say fuck." Dessie giggled. "Sounds like 'fack.' Hilarious."

He glared at her and rolled his eyes. "Oh please. Do shut up."

"Okay."

"Thank you." Marcus kept pacing and muttering to himself, his hands behind his back, looking like Napoleon at Waterloo.

Dessie suddenly jumped up. "I just thought of something!"

"What?"

"My granny. She knew people who worked at the big house when Tom Hourigan lived here. I think one of her friends was a maid in this house. She must have heard something."

Marcus stopped pacing. "Yes, that might give us a clue. Where is she now?"

"Uh, dead. In the graveyard."

"Shit."

"But she had a daughter, who's still alive. An old woman called Bridget. She used to do sewing and mending, and she lives in this little cottage near the vicarage. Why didn't I think of her before?"

"Yes, why didn't you?" Marcus muttered.

"Never mind. I just didn't. Let's go find her."

* * *

Looking for Bridget proved a futile exercise. Nobody knew where she had gone after moving out of her cottage, not even Miranda. They gave up on the day and walked back to the gatehouse. Marcus would call the firm and find out if there were any new developments about the legal dispute. Dessie decided to do a little work on her computer, transferring her notes to the catalogue file and downloading Marcus' photos. "Just in case," she said. After a few hours' work, she switched off the computer, put on her jacket and hiking boots, and headed out the door to the path up the hill. It had just stopped raining again, and she craved fresh air and exercise after having been inside for hours.

She marched up the path, the wind in her hair, taking deep gulps of the chilly air. Her mood lifted as soon as she left the outskirts of the village and could see the top of the hill ahead, where she knew she'd have stunning views of the valley and the river. When she rounded the bend, she sensed rather than heard there was someone walking behind her. She stopped and turned around. It was Rory, charging up the slope with huge strides. Dessie waved, and he increased his pace until he was beside her.

"Hi," he breathed and took off his knitted cap. "Didn't think anyone else was up here in this wind and cold."

Dessie laughed. "I couldn't stand being indoors anymore. Had to get out. Cabin fever or something."

He smiled. "Still the outdoor girl, eh? I remember you used to run around in bare feet all summer long, like a wild thing."

Dessie laughed. "Yeah, I did. I hated putting on socks and shoes when school started. But now I'm quite fond of shoes, really. Especially hiking boots."

"Yours are pretty special. Meindl no less. Must have cost a packet." Rory started walking again with Dessie beside him, trying her best to keep up with him.

"Yes, but they're not seven league boots like yours," she panted. "Could you slow down a bit? Unless you want to be alone?"

He slowed his pace and looked down at her. "No, I'd like your company. I've been so caught up with the farm accounts and all the grants stuff, I needed a blast of fresh air. Haven't talked to anyone for a while."

"Not even Jules?"

He sighed. "Oh, Jules. Yeah, well… being with her is a bit of a roller coaster ride."

"Ha," Dessie said. "I know what you mean. She's so unpredictable. You never know when she's going to lash out. It's like, tra-la-la, then wham! And you have no idea what made her so angry. Except the last time; she let me know then. Only she was wrong." Dessie felt tears welling up as the old hurt stabbed her yet again.

Rory glanced at her and took her hand in his big fist. "Your hand is cold."

"My hands are always cold."

"Cold hands, warm heart. You need gloves." He glanced at her. "Are you still upset about that guy? The one who dumped you all those years ago?"

"No. Not upset about *him*. I was lucky I didn't end up with him. I found out lately what a total bastard he really is. But what happened that summer changed my life. And I felt as if I lost a sister."

"Maybe you can get her back?"

Dessie stopped dead, making Rory stumble. She grabbed his arm to steady him. "Oh, sorry. You okay?"

"Yes, fine." He resumed walking.

Dessie half-ran beside him. "But listen, Rory. I do want to make up with Jules, I really do. But how can I? She hates me." She started to cry, tears running down her cheeks. "I loved Jules. She was my big sister, my rock. I loved Harry too," she sobbed. "The two of them were like substitute parents when Mum and Dad died. But then all that…stuff happened, and I looked to Harry for comfort, as if he were my dad, but then…" Dessie stopped and wiped her face with the back of her hand. "Well, you know what happened."

Rory pulled a crumpled but clean handkerchief from his pocket and dabbed at Dessie's face. "Don't cry, Dessie. Don't be sad. I know you're telling the truth. I didn't then, but I do now."

Dessie stopped crying and stared at him. "You do? Here, give me that." She took the hanky from him and blew her nose noisily. "You sure didn't back then. God, you have no idea how to dry a girl's tears."

"I'm sorry," Rory mumbled.

"It's okay. You tried your best. Wiping tears is a delicate task. Not for big hunky guys like you."

Rory laughed. "No, you twit, I meant I'm sorry for not

believing in you way back then. I'm sorry I didn't stand up for you and tell my mother what a lying bitch she was. I should have, but I couldn't. I was still, I dunno…"

"Under her spell?"

"Something like that," he mumbled, his face flushed. "I was a wimp. It took me until quite recently to tell her where to get off. All thanks to Finola."

Dessie stared at him. "Finola?"

"Yeah. Finola McGee. She swept in here like a white tornado and made everyone stand up and take notice. She's amazing. She has this way of making you look at yourself and who you are. She takes no prisoners, that's for sure. Scary woman."

"I've heard about her. Hotshot reporter who married a Hollywood film star. She sounds both good and bad." Dessie shivered and started to walk. "Come on, I'm getting cold. Let's go to the top and turn around."

"Good idea." Rory fell into step with Dessie.

"Anyway, I'm not mad at you anymore," Dessie said as they walked. "I forgive you. I know it was hard for you when your mother threw around all that shit about me. I'd say it was difficult not to believe it."

Rory took her hand. "Thank you. I'm glad we're friends." He paused and cleared his throat. "Way back then, I had, uh, other feelings for you."

Dessie shot a sideways glance at him. "Yeah, right. Let's forget about the old days and move on, okay? We can't change the past, but we can make sure the future is better."

"You're a wise old woman."

"Yes, that's me. Wise, and old, and bitter." Dessie pulled her hand out of his grip and walked ahead on the narrowing path. "Come on," she shouted over her shoulder. "Let's race to the top." She started to run up the rocky track, stumbling now and then but still managing to keep up a fast pace while Rory thundered behind her, his breath laboured. Not as fit as her, that's for sure. She had started to run just to get away from the feelings his words and his touch had sparked in her mind and heart. Good old Rory had suddenly turned into someone different, someone to whom she suddenly felt close. She didn't want to become attracted to him, or start some kind of romance. That would be terrible. Jules would hate her even more if…She stopped to catch her breath, then raced on, thoughts of Jules and her rage making her heart race and sweat break out. She wanted to make peace with Jules, not break up her love affair with Rory.

She reached the top of the hill and stopped, breathing hard. She bent over, put her hands on her knees, and tried to slow her breathing. That was a tough climb, and running up it had been torture. She looked around and saw Rory belting up the last bit, his face red and sweaty.

She couldn't help laughing. "Come on, ya ould geezer!"

"Are you trying to kill me?" Rory wheezed. "I'm more than ten years older than you, you know."

"Ha, that's no excuse." Dessie sat down on a rock and wiped her brow with her scarf. "I'm about to hit thirty myself."

"Just a step away from the old folks' home then." Rory wiped his face with his sleeve. "I shouldn't have given you my hanky to blow your nose."

Dessie patted the rock. "Sit down here and let the air cool you. You'll soon want to move again."

He joined her on the rock, and they looked out at the view of the valley, the rolling hills beyond, and the outline of the mountains, purple with heather, against the blue sky. The cold wind smelled of earth and woodsmoke.

Dessie breathed in deeply. "I love this smell. It takes me back to when I used to walk up this hill with Daddy and Jules. We always came up here on Sundays."

"Not Miranda?"

"No, she wasn't the outdoorsy type. She did ballet and other girly stuff. Jules and I were the tomboys."

"And now you're back, working as an auctioneer," Rory remarked. "How is it going? I bet there are some interesting things in that house."

Dessie sighed. "It's not going well at all. We've hit a huge problem. Or, I should say, a huge problem has hit us."

"What kind of problem?"

Dessie turned her head and looked into Rory's earnest grey eyes. Beautiful eyes, she noticed, with black lashes. Why had she never realised what a handsome man he was? "I'm not really allowed to say anything. But I trust you to keep this between us."

"I won't tell a soul. You don't have to share it with me, but if you need to talk to someone, I'm here."

"Thank you. Yes, I think I need to talk to someone about this. To make a long story short, there's now a dispute about ownership. Someone has come forward with claims that Tom Hourigan and his wife, Conchita, weren't married, so their children were illegitimate."

"He didn't make a will?"

"No. But as the children were then thought to be the issue of their marriage and the only heirs, there seemed to be no problem. So, they have to find the marriage certificate or records of their marriage in some parish or other." Dessie drew breath.

Rory stared at her in silence. "I see. In that case the auction won't take place? Or at least not until this has been cleared up?"

"Exactly."

"That's really bad luck."

"Yeah."

"Maybe that marriage certificate is somewhere in the house?"

"No. Ri—the house has been searched from top to bottom. They probably weren't married in Ireland because no records have been found."

Rory nodded. "That's true. They weren't."

"What?" Dessie blinked. "What do you know about this?"

"Old story. But could be true. Never thought of it much until now. You see…" Rory pushed his hand through his hair. "Let me think… There was this old woman my mother knew. She used to work at the telephone switchboard in the village in the 1930s. You know, in the old days, everyone had to go through the switchboard to make a phone call. Of course, the telephonists were not supposed to listen, or tell anyone if they heard something by accident. But of course they did, the nosy biddies."

"Yeah, yeah, go on. Get to the point. What did this old woman know about Tom and Conchita?"

"She said that Conchita and Tom met in London. She was only eighteen, he much older. She was in London with her parents on a visit. Then she met Tom at a party and they fell madly in love. But the parents wouldn't let them marry, so they ran away. Got married in Scotland. Gretna Green, I think. The telephonists heard about it during a conversation between Conchita and a friend in Dublin."

"Holy fucking shit!" Dessie yelled. "That's it!" She jumped up and hugged Rory. "There must be records there we could look up. Thank you darlin' Rory!" Jubilant, she hugged him again and kissed him on the mouth.

He froze, grabbed her arms and kissed her back, the kiss this time long and hard, before Dessie broke away. They looked at each other for a loaded moment. Then Dessie backed away without a word, and ran down the path as fast as she could.

CHAPTER 12

His mind whirling, Rory looked at Dessie's departing figure as she raced back down the track. He could still feel the imprint of her soft lips on his mouth, her slim body against his, the light floral scent she wore still lingering on his clothes. She was so lovely, so seductive, with the black hair, those dark green eyes, and the dimple beside her mouth. But not only that, her quick mind, her sense of fun, and the way she had grown into an alluring mature woman during the ten years she had been away were truly enchanting.

He sat down on the rock again staring at the mountains, as if they could tell him what to do. It was a hell of a situation—falling for Dessie when he was involved with her sister. Not that they were in a proper relationship, physical or otherwise, but he had sensed it was about to happen, and he had welcomed it. He and Jules would be a good team, even if she was hard to figure out at times. Quick to anger and very judgemental, Jules could be unfair and downright nasty when she was in a bad mood. But who was perfect? He had been alone long enough, thanks to his mother's meddling in his love affairs. Now that she was gone, he could make up his own mind. And he had. Until Dessie arrived. Rory sighed and got up, walking slowly down the path, feeling as if he had been hit by a natural disaster. A hurricane called Dessie.

* * *

Shit, shit, shit, Dessie thought as she raced down the path. *This must not happen. I must not fall for Rory and make him break up with Jules. I wanted to make peace with her, not flirt with her boyfriend. I can never be alone with Rory again. But he's so lovely, so solid and dependable. And sexy…* She stopped dead, breathing hard. Sexy? Rory? She nodded. Yes, he was. That split second when he had kissed her had been amazing. His lips, his hot breath, his strong body and his… *Stop it!* she told herself. *This must never, ever happen again.*

Dessie shook herself and started walking again. She had to stay cool and professional, do her job and stay away from Rory. He had given her a great tip and she decided to call Marcus straight away. This could turn things around, and the auction could go ahead once they found the records or the marriage certificate. A brilliant piece of news, actually. She took the phone from her pocket and dialled his number.

"Gretna Green," she said when he answered. "They were married there. Get back to that lawyer and tell him."

"Are you sure?"

"Certain. Nearly a hundred percent. I'm sure there are records."

"If that turns out to be true, I owe you again." Marcus laughed. "It'll be a weekend at The Ritz by the time I add up all your brownie points."

"Put it on my slate," Dessie replied and hung up. She resumed walking, glancing behind her to see if Rory was catching up with her. But the path was deserted, the cold wind whirling the dead leaves around and a lone crow flying overhead, its cry echoing eerily in the still landscape. The trees loomed over her, and the spits of rain felt like needles. Time to go inside and pretend it hadn't happened. If that was possible. She shivered and put her finger to her lips, knowing it would take a long time to forget that kiss.

* * *

The events of the next few days helped turn Dessie's mind away from romance. Marcus phoned his father in London about the Gretna Green lead. The lawyer got on the case, and they'd know if there was anything in the Scottish records in a few days. Martin Smythe was not thrilled with the news that Richard Hourigan had got away with some very valuable items from the house. Marcus was to contact him at once and get the items back or they would be in trouble with the law. Then, one evening, Audrey announced that Finola McGee was coming back early for Christmas with her twin daughters and that they'd be staying in the cottage on Jules' estate.

"Not sure where she's going to put everyone," Audrey muttered as they tidied away after dinner. "She's coming with two babies, a dog, and a nanny. More like a travelling circus."

Dessie put the butter in the fridge. "Didn't you say they had extended the cottage and added a bedroom and a bathroom?"

"That makes it two bedrooms in all. But I suppose the nanny will have to sleep with the babies, poor thing. How on earth will Colin fit into all that when he arrives from his latest movie set? He's filming on location in Iceland. Some kind of sci-fi action thing. He'll be exhausted and will want a little peace and quiet."

"Maybe the babies are well behaved?" Marcus suggested from the kitchen table, where he was enjoying a glass of wine from the bottle they had shared.

Audrey laughed. "Well behaved? Nah, those girls are wild. If you consider what their parents are like, you'll get the picture. Finola was home during the summer, and they had just started to walk. It was holy murder. Stay tuned for a lot of shenanigans."

"Not that I'll be seeing much of them," Dessie remarked. "If they're staying with Jules, I mean. She and I aren't exactly on friendly terms."

Audrey stared at her. "Really? Why is that?"

Dessie shrugged and picked up a saucepan. "Long story. Where do you want me to put this? Does it go in the dishwasher?"

Audrey nodded, still looking at Dessie with interest. "Yeah, shove it in. Thank God for dishwashers, eh?"

Marcus drained his glass and brought it to the sink. "I'll be off. I have a date, so don't wait up."

Audrey made a funny face. "A date? Oooh, exciting! Would you care to share?"

"No, I wouldn't," Marcus drawled. "Not with a hot journalist anyway. I'd find myself spread all over the front page in the morning."

"The front page?" Audrey chortled. "Aren't we full of ourselves? No, you wouldn't make more than a couple of paragraphs on page four in the social events section. I'll get Mary on the case at once. She does all that stuff at the paper."

"Very funny," Marcus snorted. "I'm off. Have a nice evening, ladies."

Audrey laughed and looked at Dessie when Marcus had left. "I wonder who he's dating?"

Dessie turned on the dishwasher. "He isn't dating anyone. I think he met some woman out hunting, and they were going to draw up a list of meets he could go to over the next few weeks, so he can book the same horse. Don't worry."

"Who's worried?" Audrey said and picked up the wine bottle.

"He said you were hot, didn't you hear him?"

Audrey shrugged. "Did he? I didn't notice. There is nearly half of this bottle left. You want to help me finish it?"

"Why not?" Dessie took two clean wine glasses from the china cabinet and sat down at the table. "Let's drink it in here, where it's warm and cosy. If we go into the living room, we'll have to light a fire. It's cold out tonight."

Audrey joined her at the table. "It's November. Not my favourite month." She poured wine into both glasses, pushed one across the table, and then lifted her own. "Cheers."

Dessie clinked glasses with Audrey. "Cheers, Audrey."

They sipped wine and chatted about the weather until Audrey fixed her gaze on Dessie. "So, what's this all about? This old scandal? I have heard rumours but not much that I can get a handle on."

Dessie widened her eyes. "Old scandal? What do you mean?"

CHAPTER 13

"Don't play the innocent with an old reporter," Audrey warned. "I can smell a story a mile away. Not that I'd print yours, I just want to know what's true and what's not."

Dessie pushed a breadcrumb around the table. "Not sure I want to open that particular can of worms right now. Or ever." She met Audrey's eyes, trying to gauge her sincerity and understanding. "Whatever I say gets twisted and turned."

"I won't twist anything. And I won't press you further if it's too hard for you to talk about it."

"It's okay." Dessie suddenly felt an urge to tell her story to Audrey. "It could be good to tell you."

Audrey nodded. "I'm listening."

Dessie took a deep breath, and before she knew it, she had told Audrey her story: what happened in the rose garden; the subsequent heartbreak when Richard sent her a text message saying he was leaving; the moment of despair when she had run to the stables to hide, so ashamed and miserable she wanted to die. Then how Harry had found her and comforted her and Breda Quirke seeing them and spreading those horrible lies all over town. She drew breath when she had finished her tale. "That's about it, really."

Audrey looked thoughtful while she sipped her wine. "What a total gobshite."

"I know," Dessie sighed. "I can't understand why I was so obsessed with him."

"Because he was a hot American, of course. You were only—how old?"

"Nineteen. Should have known better at that age, but I hadn't been anywhere really by then. I finished my leaving cert exams the year before, and then I worked with Miranda at her organic farm, helping her get started while I tried to decide what I really wanted to do with my life."

"So you were this beautiful, innocent country girl, dreaming about your future, when this hottie from New York rides into town?"

Dessie couldn't help laughing. "Yeah, that's about it, really. Not so innocent now, though. I lived it up at college," she added with a wink.

Audrey smiled. "Good for you. Us girls need to sow our wild oats too, don't we?"

"Not that it made me particularly happy. I was just so angry. I think I took it out on other men. I just slept around for a bit and then I'd text them and say it was over." Dessie felt a wave of shame wash over her. The bravado she'd felt when she'd told Miranda about her college years faded. She had treated those poor men badly. What would Audrey think? "Not very proud of that," she mumbled.

Audrey topped up Dessie's glass. "Not very nice, I agree. But having been run out of town by a lynch mob, so to speak, might have changed your outlook on life, and men. And yourself."

Dessie picked up her glass. "Yeah, something like that. I kind of felt that everything that happened was all my fault, and then I started to hate myself. I wanted to punish myself and become harder and stronger that way."

"Did it work?"

Dessie thought for a moment. "Yes, in a way. But I don't think it made me immune to men, or to falling in love."

Suddenly, Rory's face floated into her mind. "And if you do fall for someone, it's very hard to stop it, even if he's the last person you should love."

Audrey leaned across the table and fixed Dessie with her bright blue eyes. "I have a feeling something's going on there…"

Dessie felt her face flush. "I don't want to talk about it."

Audrey sat back. "That's okay. Of course. I'm sorry if you felt I was prying."

"No, that's okay. I'm glad I told you. Now you know what happened to me all those years ago. That's a good thing. I have a feeling a lot of people are more open to believing me now. Except for Jules."

Audrey pushed her glass away. "Jules? Stubborn woman. Very opinionated. But a true blue when the chips are down, Finola says. They're very close."

"That must be a strong friendship," Dessie said with a shiver. "Not women you'd fool with and come out alive."

Audrey giggled. "I'm sure Colin got more than he bargained for. Being married to Finola can't be a walk in the park." She paused. "But talking about men…how about Marcus? He's not the…?"

Dessie shook her head. "Nah. Not my type. I don't go for the fruity accent and the designer clothes. He's a nice guy behind it all and very decent to work with, but that's all. You're welcome to him."

"Gee, thanks." Audrey smiled wickedly. "I find him quite delicious. But I hide it."

"Not very well," Dessie countered. "But I'm sure he hasn't noticed."

"That's a relief." Audrey examined the bottle. "All gone. Shall we open another?"

Dessie pushed away her glass. "No thanks. I've had enough truth serum for tonight. If I have any more, I might get totally pissed and tell you stuff you didn't even want to know."

"That sounds scary. But you're right. Let's call it a night. I need to get my beauty sleep if I'm to hook that hot Brit."

They were interrupted by a trilling sound.

"My phone," Dessie said after a moment's confusion, and picked it up from the counter by the fridge. "Hello? What do you want? If you're selling something, we're broke."

"Dessie?" Marcus asked. "Is that you? Are you feeling okay?"

"Yes, it's me. I'm just a little...flustered. We finished the wine."

Marcus started to laugh. "Oh, yes, I noticed it was strong. Fourteen percent. Enough to floor a very big horse."

"We're not floored, we're very happy, thank you," Dessie said primly. "Whaddya want? That date not going very well?"

"It wasn't a date. It was a meeting. And she left. I'm still in the pub, and I've met some rather spiffing people, so I'll be a bit late."

"That's absolutely fine, dear chap."

"Delighted to hear it. Now listen, if you can take this in, I owe you dinner, right?"

"You certainly do," Dessie said with feeling. "With knobs on. Where are you taking me?"

"I wish," Marcus mumbled. "But seriously...there is this new gastro pub that just opened in Clonmel. I thought we could go there and try it out? And here is another suggestion. Ask Audrey if she wants to come too. What do you say?"

Dessie looked at Audrey and smiled. "That sounds like some kind of kinky threesome, but we'd love to, wouldn't we, Audrey?"

Audrey nodded. "Definitely."

"She said yes," Dessie drawled into the phone. "You'll never get a better offer."

Marcus sighed. "You two sound completely pissed. But who's complaining?"

"You got yourself a date with wonder boy," Dessie said when she had hung up.

"Not what I'd call a dream date," Audrey remarked. "But it's a start, isn't it?"

"A very good one. I think he wants you, but he hates himself for it. This way he can ogle you in secret."

Audrey laughed. "I'll ogle him right back."

* * *

The main bar of the new gastro pub in Clonmel was buzzing, but the chic dining room was nearly deserted.

"Have you reserved?" The head waiter drawled, looking at them through half-closed eyes.

"No," Marcus replied, scanning the room.

"In that case—"

"Hi, Seamus," Dessie interrupted. "It's you, isn't it? Seamus Murphy? You sat in front of me in second year. You've grown since then, and your skin's cleared up. Hardly recognised you. Hey, give us a good table, willya?"

Seamus blinked and opened his eyes fully. "Good evening, uh...?"

"Dessie. You know very well who I am," she snapped, her Tipperary accent broadening. "Come on, we haven't got all night."

"I'll have a look." Seamus consulted a clipboard on the counter. "Weeell..."

Audrey stepped from behind Marcus and Dessie. "Jesus, will you give us a table! Don't be so fecking precious. Where do you think you are? The Ritz? I'm going to review this place for the paper, you know, so..."

Seamus cleared his throat. "I can give you a table by the..." He stopped as Audrey marched across the restaurant and pulled out a chair at a table near the fireplace, where a turf fire blazed, casting a cosy glow on the polished floorboards.

"We'll be very happy here," she announced.

Seamus gave up. "Right. I'll get you some menus."

"Thanks," Dessie called after him. "The restaurant looks fantastic, by the way. And your skin too."

Laughing, Marcus sat down beside Audrey. "You two are priceless. Remind me to bring you next time I need a table in a crowded restaurant."

"Only if the head waiter is a lad from County Tipperary," Audrey said.

"I wouldn't rule that out," Dessie countered. "Tipp people are everywhere."

"Let's see what their food is like." Audrey opened the menu a waitress had handed her and scanned the long list of dishes. "Great. Not too fancy. Good country fare with a modern twist. That's clever. They even have black pudding with grainy mustard and sweet apple sauce as a starter. You should try that, Marcus. Not as filling as it looks. Then you could follow with Kerry lamb cutlets with mint jelly and pan-fried potatoes, served with rosemary flavoured puree of peas. How does that sound?"

"To a man who has spent five hours in the saddle?" Marcus quipped. "Heaven."

"I'll have that too," Dessie cut in, her stomach rumbling. "You made it sound so delicious and I forgot to have lunch today."

The restaurant slowly filled with customers. Dessie idly watched them while they waited for their orders. Most of them were couples out on a date, mixed with older people in groups. Dessie gave a start as a small group of people walked in, chatting and laughing. She vaguely recognised a few of them, but two in particular caught her attention— her sister Jules looking gorgeous in a blue top and wide black trousers and the man who followed her in...Rory, all dressed up in a suit and tie, looking faintly uncomfortable in such a trendy place.

Jules glanced around the room and caught sight of Dessie. Their eyes met. Time stood still. Then Jules walked across the floor to their table.

"Hi, Dessie."

"Eh, hi," Dessie mumbled. "Nice place they made out of the old warehouse, don't you think?"

"Fabulous." Jules glanced at Audrey. "Hi there, how are you?"

"Great, thanks," Audrey replied. She gestured at Marcus. "This is Marcus Smythe from London. Dessie's boss. Marcus, this is Juliet Thomas-Smith. Dessie's sister."

Marcus got up and shook hands with Jules. "I know. We met out hunting just a few hours ago. I hired that horse for the opening meet too. Nice to see you again. That's one hell of a horse you've got."

Jules nodded. "Thanks. He's very special." She turned to Dessie. "I…I have something I need to say to you. But not here…" She looked over her shoulder at Rory, who nodded. "Can you come to the house? Tomorrow?"

"Of course," Dessie breathed, her heart racing. "When?"

"Around seven? For supper?"

"I'll be there," Dessie promised.

Jules touched Dessie's arm. "Thank you. See you then." She walked back to join her party.

Dessie looked on as Rory pulled out a chair for Jules. He looked up, and their eyes met. Dessie smiled. Rory grinned and winked then turned his attention back to Jules. Dessie's gaze drifted to Audrey and Marcus, involved in flirty banter across the table. How lucky they were. Flirting and laughing and probably falling in love without complications. Why couldn't that happen to her? She looked at her plate of black pudding with sweet apple sauce, beautifully presented and more delicate in flavour than she had expected. She glanced at Jules' party and suddenly lost her appetite as she watched Rory put his hand on Jules' back in an intimate gesture. She was sure he had been instrumental in getting Jules to soften toward her. How kind of him. A chance to talk to Jules and perhaps regain her trust and friendship. But what about Rory? How could she hide her feelings for him? Dessie ate without tasting anything, while the candles flickered and everyone around her had a wonderful evening.

CHAPTER 14

The cataloguing continued the next day despite the lack of news from the lawyers or Smythe's.

"Might as well keep going," Marcus said. "If the records show they were married, then the auction will go ahead as planned."

Dessie agreed, and they got stuck into the dining room with its imposing mahogany sideboard full of china and silver. The pale green damask-covered walls were adorned with watercolours and big oil paintings of English land-scapes.

"Too big for that dweeb Richard to steal," Marcus mut-tered as he studied one of them. He glanced at Dessie. "You two knew each other from before, is that right?"

Dessie dropped the silver salver she had been studying. "Yes, sort of. He was here that last summer, before..."

"Before what?"

"Before I went to college." Dessie picked up the salver. "This one's early Georgian. Must be from the O'Connor period. William IV."

Marcus shifted his gaze from Dessie's hot face to the silver dish. "Put a value of five hundred and fifty on it. I'm sure it'll go for more, but it's a good starting price." He pointed at the oil. "That's a John Faulkner." He lifted the camera hanging from his neck and took a shot. "I'd say around two thousand.

It's signed too, at the lower left-hand side. Will you remember that if I add it to the computer file?"

"Okay."

Marcus looked at her again. "I have a feeling you're a little distracted today. Why don't you take a break from the cataloguing for a bit and go down and get those dresses? If the legal dispute is settled, I'd like to do that photo shoot. I'm sure those gowns need some airing and freshening up."

Dessie nodded. "Thanks. You're right, I feel a bit tired today. I'll go and see what can be done with those dresses. I'm sure Miranda can help make them look bright and fresh. And I haven't even asked her if she wants to take part in this weird fashion thing you seem so hot on."

"It'll be a terrific way of attracting attention to the auction. Make it come alive, somehow. Go on, don't just stand there staring into space. Chop, chop, old fruit. Get going."

Dessie laughed. She put the silver dish back on the sideboard, pushed her notes into her bag, and ran out of the room and down the corridor. Marcus was a good sport. Caring and generous, despite his posh mannerisms and accent. She went down the stairs to the basement and the little room beside the kitchen that had been the butler's office. She opened the trunk and took out the dresses one by one, draping the soft silk over her arm. They were wrinkled and smelled a little musty but would probably freshen up if hung outside and then carefully pressed with a warm iron. Dessie delved further into the trunk, looking for belts and scarves. She found two leather belts with gold clasps and a Hermès scarf with an exquisite pattern of peacocks and exotic flowers. Then her fingers met something hard and square at the bottom of the trunk. She picked it up. It was a scuffed leather box with "Memories" written in faint gold lettering she could just about make out. "Memories," she mumbled. "I wonder what they are?" She shook it and heard something rattle. What was in it? She tucked it carefully into her tote bag, deciding to look at it when she got back to the gatehouse.

A glum Marcus met her on the way out. "I'm taking a break too. I think we might even have to call a halt to the cataloguing."

"Why? Bad news?"

He nodded. "Yes. An e-mail from my father. There are no records of Tom and Conchita having been married in Gretna Green or anywhere else in Scotland."

Dessie stared at him. "What? But that's not possible. I was sure... I mean Rory was sure that woman had said—"

"Must have been barking up the wrong bloody tree. I never thought the ramblings of an old woman who was a telephonist eighty years ago were a reliable source of information anyway. We're back to square one now."

"Shit." Dessie lifted the dresses. "What will I do with these?"

Marcus shrugged. "Don't know. You might as well put them back."

"Okay." Dessie ran back down the stairs and carefully folded the dresses and put them back into the trunk. What a pity. She had started to look forward to the vintage fashion shoot and to wearing those wonderful silk gowns.

"What do we do now?" she asked Marcus over coffee in the gatehouse. "Pack it in and go back to London?"

"No, not yet. My dad said to stay for a bit to see what might happen. It appears that Richard is planning to do some kind of deal with this distant cousin. They might still go ahead with the auction jointly or something."

"Okay."

Marcus got up from the kitchen table. "Anyway, I'm going out for lunch. Do you need a lift anywhere?"

"Not right now, but maybe this evening? I'm going to my sister's for dinner. I could walk, but it's quite far and it'll be too dark."

"Is that the big house called Knocknagow?"

"That's it." Dessie finished her coffee and put the cup on the draining board.

"Funny names you have around here."

"The name comes from an old novel that was published in 1870 or so. By a writer called Charles Kickham. It was set right here, in this part of Tipperary. The house was built shortly afterwards, and one of Harry's ancestors decided to call the house after the novel as a tribute. Harry was my brother-in-law. He died eight years ago in a riding accident."

"I'm sorry. That's very sad."

"Yes. We all missed him terribly. Still do."

Marcus put his arm around Dessie. "I'm sure you do. I hear he was very popular in hunting circles too. A real gent, I was told."

Dessie smiled, touched by the comforting gesture. "Yes, he was. And to me, the big brother I never had."

"I'm so sorry, Des."

Dessie looked up at him. The sympathy in his eyes made a long-forgotten sorrow well up. She pulled away, afraid she'd burst into tears if he continued to be kind. "Thank you. No need to dwell on it. That only makes it worse."

"True." Marcus walked to the door. "Must go. But I'm taking Miss Smarty-pants out tonight, so we'll drop you off at your sister's on the way."

Dessie grinned. "Aw, you two. I knew you'd be perfect for each other. Sure you can cope with her? She's pretty sassy."

Marcus laughed. "I like a challenge. Don't worry about me."

"I won't."

When the door had banged shut behind Marcus, Dessie tidied away the coffee cups and decided to look at her notes at the kitchen table. Might as well catch up right there in the warm kitchen. Cat was purring on her cushion in front of the stove, and the small radio played a Mozart sonata. All was well with the world. Jules would listen this time, and they would be as close as before. Dessie picked up her tote and searched inside for her notebook and her iPad among all the bits and bobs she had put inside during the morning. Her fingers found their way to the bottom, where she came across the leather box she had found earlier. She pulled it out. It should be returned to the trunk, but what harm could it do to look inside? Dessie put the box on the table. It was scuffed and stained by mould, but it had obviously been beautiful once, covered in soft green leather with swirls of gold around the word "Memories" on the top. There was a little lock on the side, which Dessie picked easily with the help of a pin she found in a kitchen drawer. She opened the box, her hands shaking, afraid to break the delicate lid. She peered inside and breathed in sharply at the sight of the contents. A gold horseshoe and two small china figures—a bride and groom. Underneath, a piece of paper with something scribbled on it in Spanish. *De la torta de la boda.* A quick search on Google translate said what she had already guessed. "From the wedding cake." But whose? And where? Her heart beating, she delved further into the box, past a small bunch of pressed violets and some letters, to the very bottom, where she found it: a certificate, yellow with age and nearly falling apart. She whooped with joy as she read the faded text with the signatures underneath and scrabbled for her phone.

CHAPTER 15

"I've got it!" Dessie shouted. "You'll never guess."

"Wh....?" Marcus spluttered into the phone. "Sorry, I'm having lunch in a pub. Nearly spit my sandwich across the bar. What's up?"

"I found it," Dessie panted. "The wedding certificate."

"What? Is this a joke?"

"No, it's real. I found this box in the trunk with the dresses. I put it into my bag, and then I meant to put it back but I forgot, and now I found it and had a look and then I saw something…" Dessie paused for breath, staring at the piece of paper in front of her.

"Yeah, yeah, go on. The suspense is killing me."

"The wedding certificate was there, at the bottom of the box. You'll never guess where they were married."

"I'm not even going to try," Marcus said dryly. "So please, cut to the chase and put me out of my misery. Where the hell were they married?"

"Northern Ireland," Dessie exclaimed. "In a place called Castlegreen. Sounds very like Gretna Green, doesn't it? That must have been what the old woman heard. I looked it up. It's a village just east of Belfast. They must have eloped there instead of Gretna Green. Clever, huh?"

"Very. And you're a genius. Put that certificate in a safe place, and don't move until I come back, okay?"

"I'll guard it with my life. I'm not moving until you come back."

"Good. Won't be a tick. I'm just going to call the office in London." Marcus hung up.

Dessie smiled to herself as she looked at the old certificate. What a stroke of luck. This meant the auction would be going ahead and also the little vintage fashion shoot. But what about Richard? Maybe he should be told about this amazing discovery? He'd be over the moon. Dessie cast her mind back to that morning when she had caught him in the study. Nah. Let him sweat. The miserable toad had been prepared to steal to cover some of his expenses. He'd find out in time. She sighed happily. She was finally over him and what had happened. Now she could look forward with confidence and hope. And all romantic notions had to be put on hold.

* * *

The gravel crunched under Dessie's feet as she walked under the starlit sky to Jules' back door. Marcus had first driven to the front door, but Dessie told him to drive around to the back.

"Nobody uses the front door around here, except if someone has died," she explained.

"What do you mean?" he asked.

"It's an Irish country thing," Audrey said. "People who are alive use the back door, which is always open and you never knock. You just barge in and shout 'Hello.' But if there's a wake, we go in through the front door, which is also used to carry dead people out."

Marcus sighed. "You Irish are so weird. No wonder we never managed to rule you."

"It's a kind of passive resistance," Audrey said. "Takes a few hundred years, but we finally get rid of whoever tries to put the arm on us."

Marcus grinned at Audrey. "I'm looking forward to this date."

"You might regret that statement later," Audrey quipped.

Dessie opened the door. "I'll get out here. I'll walk around to the back."

"Okay," Marcus said, tearing his eyes away from Audrey to look at the front door under the pillared portico. "Nice house. I'd love to see it sometime."

"Yes, it's a lovely house, if a little dilapidated. But not for sale," Dessie remarked. "Nor the contents. Jules keeps it for her son, who's the heir to the place. But he's only fifteen, so it'll be a while before he can decide what to do with it. But I'm sure she'll show it to you if you ask. The reception rooms are beautiful."

"Great," Marcus replied. "Are you sure you're okay?"

"Positive." Dessie took a deep breath of the cold, crisp air. "I need the fresh air. You go on and have a good time."

"Thanks." Marcus waved and took off in shower of gravel.

Dessie looked at the rear lights of the Alfa Romeo disappearing down the drive and shivered, more from nerves than the cold. She pulled the suede jacket tighter and walked around the corner, not looking forward to the confrontation with Jules.

* * *

There was no confrontation after all. When Dessie rounded the corner, she found all the outside lights on, the back door open and Jules' dogs sniffing at a Renault Espace with Dublin number plates. Dessie hung back, looking around. Someone had just arrived. Someone the dogs knew, as they didn't bark. Dessie jumped as a big black dog approached, sniffing at her legs. She relaxed when he wagged his tail and licked her hand.

She bent down and ruffled his ears. "What a lovely fella. Are you one of Jules'?"

The dog looked at her adoringly with his melting brown eyes and gave her a doggie smile. Dessie crouched down and hugged him while he licked her face. "You darling," she whispered into the soft black fur. She jumped as a shadow appeared in the lit doorway.

"Jake?" the woman called. "Where did you go?"

Dessie straightened up. "He's here. I suppose this is Jake?"

The woman approached, and as she turned to the light, Dessie saw her clearly. She was tall with short dark hair, blazing blue eyes and a face full of freckles.

"Oh, there you are!" She turned her attention to Dessie. "Hi, I'm Finola. You must be Dessie. You're the spit of Miranda." She grabbed Dessie's hand in a bone-crushing handshake.

"Hi," Dessie mumbled. "Yes, I'm, eh... Finola? But I thought you weren't arriving until next week."

"I decided to come a week early. Sitting in a big house in LA alone with two toddlers was beginning to get on my nerves. We'll all have more fun here, not to mention the better air quality. My husband is away filming in Iceland, you see."

Dessie nodded. "So I heard."

Jules' dogs suddenly spotted Dessie, and charged at her, barking and growling. She shrank back and tried to hide behind the shed, but it was too late. Although they didn't attack, being surrounded by six aggressive dogs was nevertheless unnerving.

Finola came to the rescue. She waded in, pulling at the dogs, slapping down those that tried to jump on Dessie and shouting at them to get down. This had little effect, until a sharp whistle from the house made them stop and run back to the house, where Jules scolded them.

Finola's eyes met Dessie's, and they started to laugh.

"Talk about the master's voice," Finola joked. "We obviously haven't whatever puts fear into a dog."

"Dessie?" Jules called. "It's okay, they'll behave now. Come in and let them get to know you so they won't attack you next time you arrive."

"Uh, okay." Dessie walked to the door, her knees wobbling.

"Don't worry, they'll be like lambs now," Finola said, following behind. "Hey, guys, I'm sorry to have barged in on your reunion. I'll just grab some stuff, go down to the cottage, and help Linda make up beds and get us organised. Give me a shout if the girls wake up."

"Okay," Jules said, holding the door open to the little hall outside the kitchen. "Hi, Dessie. Sorry about the chaos, but Finola arrived unexpectedly."

"No problem," Dessie mumbled, standing stock-still while the four big dogs sniffed at her legs. One of them, a yellow mongrel as big as a Labrador licked her hand. The others wagged their tails and panted, as if saying sorry they had misbehaved earlier. She patted their heads, wondering why on earth Jules had so many dogs.

"She adopts any stray that comes her way," Finola said behind her. "Jules is a sucker for a pair of brown eyes. But now I hear there's a pair of grey eyes that are attracting her attention too…"

"Oh, shut up, Finola," Jules snapped from the kitchen. "Stop yakking, and come and get the bedclothes and towels."

Dessie stepped over a pile of riding boots and waxed jackets on the floor and continued into the large farmhouse kitchen that hadn't changed since she left ten years earlier. The cupboards were the same solid oak painted white with wooden knobs, the counters still the scarred pine and the AGA stove exuded the same warmth. Even the smell of woodsmoke mixed with good country cooking was exactly the same. It was like stepping back in time, and she half expected Harry to come in the door, bringing with him a gust of cold air after a day's hunting. She smiled as she remembered how he used to rub his hands together and say he was starving, and that the smell of stew was more seductive than the sight of a pair of frilly knickers.

Jules' voice cut in to her reverie. "Come on, Dessie, help Finola get the sheets into the car and then we can have our supper."

Dessie sprang to attention. "Okay. But what about Finola? Is there enough food for her?"

"Linda, my nanny and general dogsbody, is cooking a chicken in my kitchen as we speak," Finola explained. "Once we've eaten, we'll get the twins and settle them into the cottage. It'll be a bit of a squeeze, but Linda swears she doesn't mind sleeping on the couch in the living room. Thank God, she's such a good sport. Nobody else would put up with the chaos that is my life."

"If the twins are asleep, I wouldn't move them," Jules cut in. "I'll keep an eye on them."

"You're the best," Finola said and kissed Jules on the cheek. "Right, let's get moving then, Dessie, if you don't mind helping out."

"No bother," Dessie said. "I suppose the sheets are in the hot press?"

Finola laughed. "I love those Tipperary sayings. Nobody but the Irish calls the airing cupboard 'the hot press.' I'm so happy to be home."

It didn't take long to carry sheets and towels from the hot press to Finola's car, and she drove off with a wave and a promise to invite Dessie to the cottage for dinner when she was settled. She even offered Dessie the use of her second car, which was parked in Jules' garage. "I don't use it now that I have the bigger one. You might as well drive it. If there's one thing that makes you feel stranded here, it's not having your own wheels."

"But it's your Mini Cooper Roadster," Jules protested. "Your baby. Are you sure you want someone else to drive it?"

Finola shrugged. "It's just a car. I have real babies now. And they won't fit in the Cooper. In any case, it's better that it's used than sitting in your garage getting flat tyres."

"That's very kind of you, Finola," Dessie interjected. "I'll take good care of it, I promise."

Finola nodded. "Great. Jules has the keys. Got to go. See you later, guys. Give me a shout if the twins wake up."

When Finola had left, Jules and Dessie went back into the kitchen. Dessie laid the table while Jules took a small leg of lamb out of the oven, fragrant with rosemary and garlic.

Dessie sniffed hungrily. "You did a leg of lamb for me! Nobody does a leg of lamb like you."

Jules smiled and picked up a carving knife. "I remembered how you loved it. And I thought it would be a lot better than a fatted calf. I wouldn't even know how to cook one, to be honest."

Dessie laughed, touched by the warmth in Jules' eyes. It would be okay. They'd be sisters once more. Nothing could break them apart ever again. Could it?

CHAPTER 16

They ate in silence for a while, enjoying the flavour and tenderness of the lamb, the velvety potato gratin, and the buttered haricot beans. The dogs wandered in and settled in front of the stove, and the wind sent raindrops tapping against the windows. Jules had opened a bottle of wine, and they both had two glasses before Jules looked at Dessie and smiled.

"Now that we've had a little Dutch courage, maybe we should talk?"

Dessie coughed, her throat suddenly dry despite the food and wine. "I suppose. Not that I have much to say, other than what I said before I left. I'll say it again: it wasn't true."

Jules looked suddenly contrite. "I know."

"What?" Dessie spluttered. "You know? You mean...?"

"I only just...well, it was Rory, really. We had a long talk that night, after he took me home from the restaurant. He made me see how wrong I was, that I should have listened to Harry and not to the gossiping women all over town. I should have stood up for you, and then you wouldn't have had to leave. Maybe Harry would still be alive too." Jules lowered her head, her tears dropping onto her plate. "I'm really sorry, Des," she whispered.

"No, Jules!" Dessie shot up and went to her sister's side. She dropped to her knees and hugged Jules tight. "Please don't say things like that. I probably would have left anyway. I wanted to go to college and do something with my life. And I did, only it could have been under happier circumstances. Harry didn't die in that accident because of me or you. It just happened."

Jules leaned her forehead against Dessie's shoulder. "Yes, but I drove him away. We had a row, and then he stormed out and got on that horse."

"A row about me?"

"No," Jules whispered into Dessie's sweater. "About the farm, the house. He wanted to sell it, and I didn't." She lifted her head and stared at Dessie, her eyes wild and full of tears. "I love this place. I loved it more than I loved him. I never said it before, but it's true. I always wanted to live here, ever since I was a small child. Then Harry wanted to marry me and all my dreams came true. But I got *him* too, and I should have loved him the way he deserved. I always knew that. And when I heard the rumours, I thought he had turned to you..."

"But he didn't," Dessie whispered. "I turned to *him*. I had been betrayed by someone and was desperate. Harry helped me through that."

"Why didn't you come to me?"

Dessie let go of Jules and got up. "I was ashamed."

"Of what?" Jules asked, bewildered. "Oh...I see."

"Yes." Dessie sat down again and stared at her hands. "I let him...you know. Not that I didn't want to, but..."

"Who was it? Rory?"

Dessie laughed. "God, no. Rory would never...I wouldn't...I mean, I didn't fancy *him* at all then."

Jules laughed and shook her head. "Nah, he was such a nerd then. A mammy's boy."

"He sure was. But look at him now. He's grown up at last."

"Oh yes," Jules agreed, a dreamy look in her eyes. "He's suddenly turned into someone I fancy big time. But enough about me. If it wasn't him, who was it?"

Dessie took a deep breath. "It was Richard Hourigan. Remember him?"

Jules shook her head. "Vaguely. I think I met him at the summer fair, but only once. Very flash and American. So, he and you were dating?"

Dessie nodded. "Yes. Secretly. He was engaged to be married over in New York. I was silly enough to believe he'd break it off with her and marry me, but that wasn't his intention at all. He just wanted a quick fling. He disappeared very quickly once he got what he was after. All I got was a text message to say 'Sorry but I have to go. It was sweet and all that.' I never hear from him again."

"What an utter pile of shit."

"Yes, he was." Dessie shrugged. "That's all water under the bridge now. I've moved on."

Jules nodded, fiddling with her cutlery. "You seem so strong." She sat up and looked Dessie in the eyes. "I just want to say that I am so desperately sorry for not believing you then. For not standing up for you instead of chanting with the chorus."

Dessie was going to say something, but Jules put out her hand. "No. Please. Don't say it was understandable or that I was having problems. There was no excuse for me to behave like that, none at all."

"I agree," Dessie said. "There wasn't. But we're sisters, and we have to stick together. Not only that, I do love you, Jules. Always have and always will. And I truly forgive you."

Jules let out a long sigh, her shoulders slumped. "Oh, sweetheart, that's so wonderful to hear. I love you too." She buried her face in her hands and started to cry, the tears seeping through her fingers. "I'm so happy," she sobbed. "So glad we finally could talk and make up." She lifted her tear-stained face. "Thank you."

"It's okay." Dessie blinked away her own tears. "We're

fine. Let's move on. Blow your nose and make me a cup of tea, willya?"

Jules let out a laugh. "Yeah, that's the best remedy." She got up and took Dessie's plate. "More wine? We might as well finish the bottle. It's from the wine cellar. One of Harry's best. Thought we'd include him in our little cryfest."

Dessie smiled, relieved Jules was back to her acerbic self. "Sure, why not? I'm not planning to drive tonight."

Jules froze on her way to the sink. "Shit."

"What?"

"I've been drinking too. I can't drive you home. And in any case, the twins are here. There hasn't been a squeak from the baby alarm, so they must be out for the count. Probably jet-lagged, poor babies."

"Oh. So how am I going to get back?"

"You want to stay the night?"

Dessie thought for a moment. "Thanks, but I need to get back. I promised Marcus we'd be up early to get back to the work on the house. And I told Audrey I'd feed Cat."

"Cat?"

"Her cat called Cat. Don't ask."

"That's funny. What about Audrey and Marcus?"

Dessie shook her head. "No. They're out on a date. I wouldn't want to disturb them."

Jules put the plates in the sink with a clatter that made the dogs jump up. "I know. We'll call Rory. I know he isn't drinking, because he was going to a committee meeting with the Farmers' Association. He should be home now. He'll drive you back."

"Are you sure?"

"Of course." Jules winked. "Rory and I are getting to be very close, if you see what I mean. He'd do anything for me."

Before Dessie had a chance to reply, Jules picked up her phone and punched in a number. After a quick few words, she hung up. "There. He'll be here in twenty minutes. I'll make tea for all three of us. Problem solved."

"Great," Dessie said, trying to look cheerful. She turned, pretending to look at a poster for horse equipment while cold sweat broke out in her armpits. *Stay cool*, she told herself. *Don't let your feelings for him shatter the peace.*

CHAPTER 17

They were silent during the short drive to the gatehouse. Painfully aware of Rory's wide shoulders touching hers and that special smell of soap mingled with horse she had come to love, Dessie stared straight ahead into the dark, wet night. The swishing of windscreen wipers and the odd ping of raindrops against the windows were the only sounds. She glanced sideways at Rory. His jaw was clenched, and his hands gripped the steering wheel as if his life depended on it.

"Thank you for driving me home," Dessie said in an effort to defuse the tension.

"You're welcome."

"Filthy night."

"Horrible."

"Thank you," she said again. "For talking to Jules, I mean. She and I had a long talk. Not easy, but now we're friends again. I'm really happy about that."

He nodded. "Me too."

They fell silent again as they passed through the entrance gates. Relieved the drive would soon be over, Dessie relaxed and put her hand on the door, ready to get out as fast as she could. But when the car stopped, she found she couldn't move.

"We're here," Rory said, still gripping the wheel.

"I know."

He groped for his door handle. "I'll help you out."

She put her hand on his arm. "No. It's okay. I'll manage."

Her touch made him stiffen, and he turned to face her. "This is one hell of a situation."

She snatched her hand back. "Yes."

He looked deep into her eyes in the gloom. "What the hell are we going to do, Dessie? And don't pretend you don't know what I mean."

"I don't know what to do," she whispered, wringing her hands in her lap.

He touched her cheek. "I know this will sound strange, but…I'm falling in love with you."

"What? How can you say that after such a short time?"

"It happened so fast, my head is still spinning. It feels scary in a way. But I do know I'm in love with you."

She looked up at him, at his beautiful grey eyes so full of fear. She caught his hand and pressed her lips to it. "Me too," she replied in a barely audible whisper. She meant to sit back, but before she knew what was happening, she was in his arms and he was kissing her so hard her mouth hurt. She opened her lips, and his tongue found its way inside while she pressed her body to his. He opened her jacket and slid his hands around her waist, finding her skin under her sweater. Dessie let herself savour the feeling of his warm hands for a moment before she tore away from him. "Oh God, Rory. We can't. Jules…"

They looked at each other in mutual despair. Rory straightened up and hit the steering wheel with the palm of his hand. "Shit! I can't stand this. I just can't stand it," he almost sobbed. "It feels just like all the other times, except this time it's worse. I'm not allowed to love you because of another woman. Is that fair?"

"No," Dessie sighed. "But we just can't do this right now. It would hurt Jules and make her hate me all over again."

"I know, I know. Jesus, this is terrible. But we have to fix it."

"How?" Dessie exclaimed. "I think Jules is in love with you. And she thinks you feel the same about her."

He sighed and took her hands. "Yes, I know. Maybe if I let her know she and I could never be more than friends, it would be a start?"

"I don't know. Jules is no fool. She'll find out the truth sooner or later."

He nodded, his face grim. "I know. But you know what? I don't care." He increased the grip on her hands. "Dessie, I need you. I want us to get married and be together for the rest of our lives. I want you in my life, on the farm, in my house, and wherever else I am. I just want you to be there."

Dessie stared at him. "On the farm? You mean give up my job and move back here?"

He looked confused. "Of course. What else would you do?"

She pulled her hands away. "Why should I be the one to move? Why don't you sell the farm and move to London with me? Why is it always the woman who has to change her life to suit a man?"

He put his fingers on her mouth. "Please, shut up. You know that wouldn't work. But let's not argue about the details. We'll work it out. You could live in London and commute here at weekends or whatever. I don't really care as long as we're together."

Dessie closed her eyes and tried to pull herself together. She had never thought of giving up her job for someone she loved. How could he expect that? She should stand up for herself and tell him she wasn't prepared to sacrifice all she'd worked for. But his fingers touching her mouth and his eyes looking into hers took her breath away and turned her brain into mush.

He leaned his forehead against hers. "We have to tell her. We have the right to be happy, to be together."

Dessie sat up. Hot fire burned in her chest. "Yes, we bloody do! We haven't done anything wrong—yet."

Rory laughed. "I want to do everything wrong with you. I want to be mad, bad, and dangerous with you and tell them all to fuck off. But let's take it slow and easy for now. Let's keep this secret until the time is right."

"I suppose we have to. I feel kind of dizzy right now. It's like a sudden hurricane hit and turned my life upside down." She smiled and ruffled his thick brown hair. "Hurricane Rory."

"Let's go away for the weekend."

"Oh, yes," Dessie sighed. "That would be heaven. But I only have Saturday and half of Sunday. We have to get this cataloguing done in time for the auction. There is so much stuff yet to get down on the lists. But Marcus is hunting on Saturday, so then we can sneak off somewhere. Not too far, though. Just one night away."

He looked at her thoughtfully. "Okay. I'll think of a nice place where we don't risk bumping into someone from town."

"Great." Dessie opened her door. "Got to go. We can't sit here all night. Don't get out." She put her hands in the air. "And don't kiss me or touch me, or I'll never get out of here."

Rory smiled. "All right, I won't. Sleep well, Dessie. I'll call you tomorrow."

Dessie clambered out of the jeep. "Bye, sweetheart," she whispered before she closed the door.

A car drove up behind them. "Must be Audrey and Marcus," Rory said and started the engine. He waved, smiled, and drove off while Dessie ran into the house and softly closed the door. Better not disturb those two after a romantic evening.

But the ensuing shouting match in the hall sounded anything but romantic. Despite two closed doors, Dessie could hear them clearly.

"But I *told* you it wasn't about the money," Marcus shouted.

"When anyone says it isn't about the money, IT'S ABOUT THE FUCKING MONEY," Audrey yelled back. "And stop calling me a feminist, you chauvinist pig!"

"But that's what you are."

"It was men like you who started the whole feminist movement. There wouldn't have to *be* any feminists if it weren't for the way you treat us."

"Oh please," Marcus grunted. "Don't make me responsible for what happened a hundred years ago."

"Nothing has changed since then," Audrey snapped. Her high heels clicked on the floor as she walked across the hall. "I'm going to bed. Goodnight."

"Hang on a sec," Marcus protested.

Dessie could hear his footsteps coming closer. Audrey murmured some kind of protest. Then Marcus said, "You're so cute when you're wound up."

"Shut up," Audrey said, but there was laughter in her voice.

"Okay," Marcus replied.

Rustling and giggles. The stairs creaked as they made their way up to Marcus' room. Mumbled words from Audrey. Then the door closed and there was silence for a long time, until the creaking of bedsprings made Dessie laugh as she undressed. At least someone got lucky tonight.

* * *

Murphy's Country house B+B, Clonakilty. C U there Saturday. Will send directions. Rory x, the text message said on Dessie's phone the following day. Feeling like the heroine in a spy movie, Dessie deleted the message as soon as she got it. Clonakilty. About two hours away. It would be fun to drive Finola's amazing car on those roads in County Cork. Saturday was only two days off. So soon. Her stomach flipped as she thought of a night with Rory.

"A pair of bronze and gilt equestrian groups, on an oval black lacquered base," Marcus voice said in her ear. "About fifteen hundred euros. What do you think?"

Dessie didn't reply, her mind still on the night with Rory. What to wear? Sexy lingerie? Would that be too obvious?

"Hello?" Marcus tapped her on the shoulder. "What price will I note down? We'll have to write down the measurements too, but I forgot my measuring tape. Did you bring one?"

Dessie blinked. "What? Oh, the bronzes." She slowly came back to the present and forced herself to concentrate, staring at the pair of bronze figures. "These are Guillaume Cousteau, seventeenth century. Could be copies, but they look the real thing. Put at least two thousand as a starting price. I think they're about twenty-four inches high, but we'll have to measure."

Marcus breathed out noisily. "Thank God you're back from whatever daydream you were in. Very impressive. You have a memory like a steel trap. No wonder the pater is so impressed with you. I think he'll make you director one day, you know."

Dessie stared at him. "Director? Me? That would be incredible." Her heart beat faster at the thought of it. Oh yes, it would be incredible. But what about Rory? What about his near proposal? Dessie suddenly realised she was facing an obstacle to her budding relationship far more formidable than Jules.

* * *

The Country House B+B just outside the picturesque town of Clonakilty was not as grand as the name suggested. It was a ramshackle pile of bricks that had definitely seen better days, possibly in the last century. The steps to the front door under a crumbling portico were cracked and broken, and the pillars were covered in moss and ivy. *You could say a lot of things about this hotel*, Dessie thought, *but charming isn't one of them.*

"It looked great on the website," Rory said after having kissed her on the cheek in the dark lobby. "But the room's okay. In fact, it's not too bad at all. En-suite and everything."

"Fabulous," Dessie said, relieved he had already checked them in. She took his hand. "I don't care if it's a tent. I'd sleep anywhere with you." Feeling awkward, she blushed and busied herself with her overnight bag. What a thing to say. Why make it so obvious?

Rory smiled. "Yeah, me too," he whispered in her ear. "Let's go to the room. Except if you're hungry?"

She handed him her bag. "It's three in the afternoon. I had lunch on the way here."

"We can have dinner in Clonakilty later." He took her bag and pulled her up the winding staircase, half-running, the steps creaking loudly as they went. They came to a stop outside a door with a big brass handle. Rory took out a key and unlocked it, pulling Dessie into the room and banging the door shut behind them. "Here we are," he said and dropped her bag on the floor.

Suddenly unable to meet his eyes, Dessie looked around the large room. A weak winter sun shone through the old sash window, where threadbare curtains fluttered in the chilly breeze. The wide oak floorboards were partly covered by a faded Indian carpet. The bed was a four-poster, made up with lace-edged sheets and feather pillows piled high against the headboard. There was a faint smell of lavender and beeswax polish. "It's a nice room," she said. "Really sweet."

Rory nodded and closed the window. "Better than the lobby, in any case."

"Much better. Excuse me for a moment." Dessie threw her coat on the bed, opened the door to the bathroom and went inside. The old roll top bathtub and outdated sink had the same seedy charm as the room and were just as clean and fresh. She washed her hands and sprayed on some eau de cologne before stepping outside again. Rory hung Dessie's coat in the old oak wardrobe and walked to meet her.

He took her hands. "This is a bit...you know, awkward. The other day, in the car, I would have thrown you in the back seat and made wild, passionate love to you. But here, with that bed..."

Dessie laughed, pulled him across the room, and pushed him onto the bed, throwing herself on top of him. "There. Now we're on the bed. What you gonna do about it, big boy?"

He threw his arms around her and squeezed her so tight she couldn't breathe. "Oh, Dessie," he groaned into her hair. They rolled around, Dessie pinned underneath him, and their lips met. She closed her eyes as his tongue entered her mouth in a deep kiss that lasted until they were both breathless. Without speaking, they looked into each other's eyes, while they struggled out of their clothes and crawled under the soft duvet.

"Linen sheets," Dessie mumbled. "How posh."

"Shut up and kiss me again," Rory ordered.

And she did, while he discovered the delights of her body with his hands, followed by his mouth. Dessie marvelled at his light touch and expert mouth, his strong, firm body, his sweet expression, and his many ways of making her feel wanted and loved. The mattress quivered while they moved, the bedsprings squeaked, and their moans echoed across the room as they consummated their newfound love.

Afterwards, Dessie lay in a rosy glow, smiling into Rory's tender eyes. "Sweetheart," she mumbled and touched his face.

"You're beautiful," he whispered.

"So are you."

"I love you."

Dessie sighed. "I love you too."

"I'll never let you go. If you take off, I'll follow you. To the ends of the earth. Even to London."

"That would be a huge sacrifice. I couldn't ask you to do that. It would be like…like clipping your wings or cutting off your manhood."

"But asking you to stay would be cutting off yours, I mean your…womanhood."

Dessie giggled. "That's sounds weird. But you know, women are different. Stronger. More adaptable. I'm sure we can find a solution. Don't worry, I won't ask you to give up the farm. That would be cruel. Unfair to even ask you to choose."

His eyes softened. "Dessie, you're…sublime."

She pulled back. "No, I'm not. Please, darling, wonderful, perfect Rory, don't put me on a pedestal. I'm a crazy, bad woman, and not the pure young girl you fancied all those years ago."

"I don't care."

"You might if you knew the truth. I wasn't a very good girl at college."

"I don't want to know what you did at college. I was a politician once, remember? I had a secret life in Dublin in those days, away from Cloughmichael and my mother. I wasn't exactly the model of good behaviour either, but nobody knows about that part of my life—except the women. And who knows? One of them might step forward and point the finger one day. Scream sexual harassment or something. I was a love 'em and leave 'em kinda guy in those days. Not very nice, I suppose."

Dessie stared at him. "I find that hard to believe. But I think I know why you acted like that. You were angry with your mother, and even yourself. But you ended up taking it out on those poor women."

"Something like that. Except they weren't poor. Nor did they suffer. Most of those relationships were conducted with a mutual understanding. The world of politics is dirty."

"But sexy? I always thought power was very sexy."

"Yes. But it's all about the quick fuck, for the sake of gratification, or to get favours or position."

"But fun, eh?" Dessie winked. "Please don't be prissy and say it was hard and cruel."

He turned on his back and laughed. "Yeah, it was fun. If you're young and ambitious and get close to the action in politics, the sex and drinking give you a buzz that can hook you big time."

"And when you lost your seat it was all over?"

He sighed. "In about three seconds."

"Must have been tough. No more women throwing themselves at you."

"That was a bit of a shock. But I got used to it."

"Very brave of you."

He pulled her hair. "When you've finished laughing at me, maybe we should get up and get out for a while?"

Dessie got out of bed. "I'm going to have a quick shower. Then maybe we could go and have a look at the town? I've never been to Clonakilty."

"Great idea."

"Finola lent me her amazing little car. Let's take it for a spin."

"Are you a good driver?"

Dessie smiled wickedly. "I'm a brilliant driver. But I like speed. Hang on to your hat, sweetheart, this ride could make your hair blow off."

Rory laughed and jumped out of bed. "I have a feeling that goes for more than a ride in that car."

CHAPTER 18

The breathtaking drive down the winding country roads around West Cork was the first of many secret outings during the next few weeks. They would meet somewhere safe, like the parking lot of a big supermarket, and then Rory would jump into the Roadster and tell Dessie to "Rev her up," and they'd take off somewhere new each time: a B+B in a hidden village, or a country hotel way off the beaten track. The accommodation was often less than elegant—ranging from shabby to downright seedy. Dessie didn't care about the nylon sheets and rubber pillows, shrugged at dingy wallpaper and candlewick bedspreads, and laughed at rickety beds and threadbare carpets. Their secret rendezvous were exciting, and she didn't want them to stop.

"We need to have it out with Jules," Rory said one evening as he looked at her in the dim light of the energy-saving light bulb of the room they had just checked in to. "I want to be able to tell my family and friends about us. I want to be a couple, and I want to buy you a ring and have an engagement party."

"Don't be so conventional." Dessie laughed and pushed him down on the bed, straddling him as she pulled off her sweater. "I love our secret trysts. Why can't we keep going like this for a bit longer?"

He sat up and pushed her off him. "Because I'm beginning to get tired of these awful hotels. This one smells of cabbage and cat pee. Can't we at least go a bit upmarket?"

She sat back on her heels. "And blow our cover?"

"We won't if we're careful."

She looked at his miserable face and felt a stab of guilt. This wasn't fun for him anymore, and maybe it never was. He had put up with the sleazy conditions for her. "Okay," she said. "Let's get out of here and look for something better."

"That wouldn't be too hard," he muttered.

"But not a word to Jules until after the auction, okay?"

He nodded. "That's only two weeks away."

"I know. But I don't want anything to get in the way of that. And it will give us a chance to prepare ourselves for the confrontation with Jules."

"We'll have to talk about that." He got off the bed and picked up his phone. "But first, I'm going to find a better hotel for tonight."

"Yes, one where they won't think it's strange that we have no luggage."

He looked up from his phone with the ghost of a smile. "This one won't care if we check in naked, as long as we show them our credit cards."

"Which one's that?"

"Mount Juliet."

Dessie gasped. "You're kidding!"

"No. I've just booked us a suite there online. Easy-peasy."

"And a zillion euros a night, no doubt."

"We're worth it. And I've just made a lot of money selling two horses. So it's my treat and no arguments."

"I wouldn't dare. Great choice, if we're going all posh. We won't risk running into anyone from Cloughmichael." Dessie put on her jacket. "Let's get out of here. Clandestine meetings in dingy hotels just lost their charm. Let's be secret in comfort."

"Now you're talking." Rory laughed.

They checked out, paid the bill, got in the car and drove the short distance to Mount Juliet, one of the most exclusive country house hotels in Ireland. Dessie felt a new kind of excitement as they swept through the gates and came to a stop outside the grand entrance. A porter rushed out and offered to take their bags and park their car. He didn't raise an eyebrow when he was told they had no luggage; he simply took the keys Dessie handed him and drove off. She looked up at the pillars and beautiful windows as they walked up the front steps. "Amazing place."

"Wonderful," Rory agreed. "And they'll be very discreet."

The staff might have been discreet, but they couldn't prevent Dessie and Rory running into a group from The Kilkenny Hunt coming out of the dining room.

One of the women stared at Dessie. "Miranda?" she asked. "Miranda Murphy?"

Dessie froze and stared back at the woman. "Eh, no. You must be mistaken."

The woman looked confused. "Oh, I'm so sorry. It's just that you look so like someone I know from Cloughmichael." Her gaze drifted to Rory. "And—? Have we met before?"

"No, I'm sure we haven't," Rory replied in a fake English accent.

Dessie laughed. "This is rather amusing. We must look like Irish people, Rupert, dahling," she said, aping his accent.

"What fun, har, har," Rory drawled.

"I'm so sorry," the woman said. "I didn't mean to be rude."

"Of course not," Dessie gushed. "I quite understand. Just a frightful mix-up, eh?" She waved her hand like royalty on a state visit. "Must dash. Cheerio."

They didn't speak until they were safely inside the suite.

Dessie collapsed onto the huge bed, laughing. "Holy shit! What a performance."

Rory didn't join in. "It'll be all over town tomorrow."

Dessie sat up. "What? Why? She bought the whole story."

"I don't think so. I could see her staring at us as we went into the lift."

"Who is she? Not from Cloughmichael, right?"

"Susan Swift. Her husband is the chairman of The Kilkenny Hunt. I've met him a few times on hunting business. I never really met her, just seen her from a distance at the hunt ball last February."

"She didn't seem to know who you were."

"It might come to her in the middle of the night."

"Maybe it won't." Dessie touched his cheek. "Come on, let's enjoy this sumptuous suite and forget about Susan Whatshername."

"We can't go down to dinner," Rory said glumly.

"So what? We'll order room service. Cheer up, sweetie. It won't happen. And if it does, we'll cross that bridge when we come to it, okay?"

Rory relaxed and threw his tweed jacket on a chair. "Okay, my darling, let's enjoy ourselves."

But it wasn't as much fun as they had hoped. A cloud seemed to hover over them as they made love in the huge four-poster bed, wallowed in the enormous bathtub drinking champagne, and, dressed in the fluffy hotel bathrobes, ate fillet steak and gratin dauphinois with petits pois brought by a waiter who smiled benignly at them, as if they were a honeymoon couple.

"The sleazy hotels were more fun," Dessie sighed as they got ready for bed. "I probably wasn't made for a life of luxury."

"I just want this to end," Rory said from the depths of the pillows. "Then you can sleep in my bed."

"And you in mine."

"There'll be a lot of hassle before that happens," Rory said dolefully.

"I know. It'll get worse before it gets better," Dessie replied, crawling in beside him. She closed her eyes as he put his arms around her. "We might have to cool it for a bit," she mumbled. "Just until we can sort everything out with Jules."

He didn't reply. His even breathing told her he was asleep. She stared into the darkness and wondered how on earth she was going to tell Jules.

* * *

They did the photo shoot the following day. It was a cool autumn morning with mist floating around trees and shrubs. Dan declared the light "perfect for that thirties feel." Miranda and Dessie shivered in the silk dresses, looking alternately pensive and wistful, wandering around the garden, posing beside bushes and flowerpots and draping themselves on the low parapet on the terrace. The house and its crumbling garden ornaments made perfect backdrops for the pictures that would be featured in the weekend edition of The Irish Times in an article about the house and the auction. They went inside and posed some more, in the drawing room and library, lounging on the silk-upholstered sofas pretending to read the leather-bound books, or sipping pretend tea from paper-thin china cups.

Miranda loved the dresses and said she would put in a bid for each one, hoping she'd be able to afford them. "They're still in good nick," she said, lifting the hem of the ivory silk gown. "I can't imagine anything more perfect for the hunt ball. You should go, and wear the blue one, Dessie."

"When's the hunt ball? I know The Kilkenny Hunt have theirs in February."

"The Cloughmichael hunt ball is usually after theirs. At the end of that month. We could go to both."

"I'll be…" Dessie stopped. "I don't know where I'll be then."

Miranda frowned. "Back in London, I thought, no?"

Dessie looked away. "Probably. But who knows? Life's strange."

"It certainly is," Miranda remarked, an edge in her voice.

Dessie looked at her. "What's up? You look worried."

Miranda got up from the sofa and glanced at the door. "Can he hear us?"

"Who? Dan? No, I think he left. I heard the door slam. He wants to get the photos off to The Irish Times as soon as he's edited them."

Miranda relaxed and sat down again. "Oh. Okay." She fiddled with the silk belt. "It's Jules. She's said some strange things to me."

"Like what?"

Miranda met Dessie's eyes. "She accused me of having an affair. She said some woman had called her and said I was at Mount Juliet with a very handsome Englishman last weekend."

Dessie gasped. "What?"

"You heard."

Dessie suddenly found it hard to breathe. This was awful. That woman must have talked to Jules but got it all wrong. Miranda with a handsome…Englishman? Rory must have been a very convincing British toff. If it weren't so terrible, she'd laugh. "Holy shit," she whispered.

"I know. What the hell is wrong with Jules? I had to tell her we were all in Kerry that weekend. I even had to get Jerry to talk to her before she believed me."

"Oh my God," Dessie mumbled.

"What's the matter?" Miranda asked. "You're as white as a sheet."

Dessie got up. "I'm cold. Let's get out of these frocks and go and make some hot tea in the gatehouse. I can't understand how women in the old days didn't die of pneumonia wearing these flimsy garments in the middle of winter."

"They probably wore thick woolly vests underneath."

Dessie smiled. "How sexy."

Miranda shivered. "Wish I was wearing one of these right now. I'm not prepared to catch pneumonia to look pretty."

Dessie laughed. "Nor me. You're right, it's freezing. Come on. Let's get out of here. But the shoot was fun. Can't wait to see the feature."

"Yes, that'll be exciting. We'll be famous," Miranda said, laughing.

"Not too famous, I hope," Dessie added, wondering if *that* woman read The Irish Times.

CHAPTER 19

The feature in The Irish Times was stunning. The photos of Miranda and Dessie were beautiful and evocative with a wistful, nostalgic air that would capture the imagination of many readers.

"They're like real 1930s photos," Audrey remarked as she read the weekend magazine at the kitchen table. "It's amazing how black-and-white photos are much more realistic than colour."

Marcus looked at the photos over Audrey's shoulder. "He's a damned good photographer. The photos have a sad air, as if the women in them are long gone." He smiled at Dessie sitting at the opposite end. "You and your sister are very good models."

Dessie shrugged. "It was nothing we did. It was the place, the mist, the house, and all those things in it. I felt as if I'd gone back in time. It was a little spooky, to be honest."

Audrey nodded and turned the page. "And here's the piece about the house and the whole story of the family. This should make the auction big news."

"Just as I planned," Marcus said. He picked up his plate and cup. "I'll be off."

"Hunting?" Audrey asked.

"It's Saturday," Marcus replied.

"Of course," Audrey snapped. "Why did I ask?"

Marcus glanced at her. "Yes, why did you?"

Audrey shrugged. "Just for fun. Have a good day. See you at the pub tonight?"

"I'll let you know. Bye, Dessie. See you at the house tomorrow. We're starting on the upstairs rooms, remember?"

"What's going on with you two?" Dessie asked when Marcus had left. "Do I sense a little tension there?"

Audrey looked down at her plate. "Don't know. He's difficult to figure out." She looked up at Dessie. "But maybe I am too." She sighed and helped herself to a slice of soda bread from the basket. "It's complicated. We're so different. We get along, sure, and we have fun conversations." She let out a laugh. "And in bed, he's amazing. You'd think he was Italian or something."

"That's a start, isn't it? I mean, if you get on in bed…" Dessie's thoughts strayed to Rory and his remarkable skills in that area.

Audrey looked thoughtful. "I suppose that's important, if all you want is a fling. But if you're hoping for something more than that…" She stopped and stuffed the rest of her bread into her mouth. "Never mind," she said when she'd swallowed. "Maybe it's better not to think too much. Just enjoy it while it lasts?"

"I can't answer that," Dessie replied. "Either way, it ends in tears. Always does."

Audrey nodded. "Except if you find that 'until death do us part' guy. And if you do, hang on to him and never let him go."

"Even if it means having to give up your career or move away from home?"

"You sound as if you're asking yourself the question."

Dessie fixed Audrey with her gaze. "I might have been, but now I'm asking *you*."

Audrey was silent for a long while. "Yes," she finally said. "I would give up my career and move to wherever he wanted if it was the real thing, that forever love."

"Why is it always the woman who has to give things up?" Dessie moaned.

"Not always, but more often than not." Audrey got up. "That's just the way it is, baby."

Dessie let out a sad little laugh. "Yeah. I know."

"I'm going out. You want to come for a walk in the mountains? It's cold but nice."

Dessie opened the magazine. "Thanks, but I want to read this and have another cup of tea. Just laze around for a bit, you know?"

"Good idea. See you later. Are you in for dinner?"

"Not sure yet, but I'll let you know."

"Great. See ya later."

Just as the door slammed shut behind Audrey, Dessie's phone beeped. It was a text message from Jules. **Need to talk now!**

Dessie gulped. This was it. Jules had found out. She punched in Jules' number but only got her voicemail. Only one thing to do. Go over there and face the firing squad.

* * *

There was no firing squad, or even any sign of something brewing. Dessie found Jules mucking out the stables, the dogs lying in the straw, the radio playing a cheery song and Jules singing along out of tune.

She looked up when Dessie stuck her head into one of the loose boxes. "Hi. Thanks for coming."

"No hunting today?"

"Nah, my hunter lost a shoe yesterday, and I couldn't get the farrier out in time. Grab that shovel and gimme a hand, willya?"

Dessie shrank back from the smell of horse manure. "You want me to muck out?"

"Yeah. It's not as if you haven't done it before. Come on, don't just stand there looking prissy. Or have you forgotten how?"

"Well, I…" Dessie grabbed the shovel, happy she had decided to wear wellies in case of rain. "Okay. I'll show you I can do it." She pushed the shovel into the pile of manure and straw and lifted it into the wheelbarrow. "There."

"Great stuff." Jules said, laughing. "Keep going. It'd be good if we could have all the stalls done before lunch."

"How many are there?" Dessie grunted, lifting another shovel.

"Six left. I've done two already." Jules turned the radio up. "We can sing while we work. Remember how we used to do that?"

"Yeah, when all I had was one pony to clean up after, not eight hunters."

"Ah, come on, let's do it together." Jules started belting out "Mama Mia" along with Abba.

Dessie laughed and joined in. It would be okay. Jules couldn't possibly know about Rory. It had to be something trivial, or did she just want help mucking out? "So, what was it you needed to talk about?" she asked as they washed up in the tack room.

Jules dried her hands on a rag. "Oh, it was about this woman. Awful gossip, but very observant."

Dessie soaped her hands. "Yes?"

"Well, she…" Jules stopped. "None of my business, of course. You're an adult and all that."

Dessie glanced at Jules. "But…?"

"But she said she saw you at Mount Juliet with a man. An Englishman." Jules coloured. "At first, she said it was Miranda, so I rang her up and accused her of having an affair. Shit, that was embarrassing. Jerry didn't think much of that and gave me an awful roasting. So, of course, I thought the woman—her name is Susan Swift—was mistaken. But then she called me this morning and said she had seen the feature with you and Miranda in The Irish Times and realised she'd mixed you up." Jules drew breath.

Dessie blinked. "Oh. Okay."

Jules handed her the rag. "Here. Dry your hands."

"Thanks." Dessie dried her hands for a full minute while Jules looked at her expectantly.

"So...?" Jules finally said.

Dessie turned her head and looked at Jules coolly. "So?"

"Were you? At Mount Juliet? With a good-looking Englishman? Is it that Marcus guy who hunts with our pack?"

Dessie smiled mysteriously. "Wouldn't you love to know?"

Jules sighed. "Yes, I would. Everyone in the hunt is swooning about him. I'd love to tell them my sister is dating him."

"No, I'm not," Dessie said, feeling it was the only true thing she had said since she arrived.

Jules looked confused. "Who was it, then?" Her face darkened. "He's married? Is that it?"

"No. He's not married."

"In that case, what's the problem?"

Suddenly, something snapped in Dessie. She sank down on a pile of straw and started to cry. "I can't do this anymore," she sobbed. "I can't go on lying and hiding, I have to tell you."

Jules stared at her. "Tell me what?"

"That the man that woman saw me with is...is Rory." Dessie hid her face in her hands, unable to meet Jules' shocked eyes. "I'm sorry, Jules. Really, really sorry. It just happened. We met out walking one day, and then we met again a couple of times, and all along, I tried my best not to fall in love with him. But I couldn't stop myself. Or him. We're in love, and I know this is it, it's for keeps." Dessie kept her eyes on the flags of the tack room floor while she rummaged in her pocket for a hanky.

Jules was silent while Dessie dabbed her eyes and blew her nose.

Dessie finally looked at her sister, who stared back at her with cold eyes. "Right, okay. Now I know. Thank you for telling me."

"Are you upset?"

Jules eyes turned hard. "You're damn right I'm bloody upset. You must have known Rory and I were…that well, we were getting close. Did he tell you that?"

"He said he likes you a lot, but that he didn't feel…" Dessie stopped, trying to find words that would soften the blow. "He admires you. He thinks you're very attractive. He said you had a great friendship going, but that's all."

Jules leaned against the rack of saddles and crossed her arms. "Yeah, right, bollocks. If he thought we were just friends, why all the sneaking around? A friend would tell another friend about falling in love. But he must have known there was something else there, something deeper, only waiting to happen, until you waltzed back into town and winked at him."

"I didn't wink at him," Dessie protested.

Jules shrugged. "Yeah, well, whatever. So, now I know. Thanks for telling me. Now could you leave, please?"

Dessie got up and touched Jules' arm. "Listen, I'm really sorry. I didn't do it on purpose to hurt you. It just—"

"— happened, yeah I know. But I need to be alone. I can't bear to look at you."

Dessie shrank from Jules' angry eyes. "Okay. I hope you can find it in your heart to forgive me."

Jules nodded. "Maybe. But right now, I can't."

"That's okay. I understand, I really do."

"Good. I might talk to you about it one day. But that rat, Rory? I'll never forgive him, the slimy bastard."

* * *

"She called you a rat and a slimy bastard," Dessie told Rory over a beer at the pub later that day.

Rory let out a sound between a groan and a laugh. "Yeah, I'm sure she did. But you know what? I never said anything or made any sign that there was something more between us than friendship. It was all in her imagination. Yes, okay, we've seen each other a lot, and she cooked me dinner and did her hair and put on make-up. Made her look a hell of a lot more attractive, I have to say. She's a good-looking woman, but you can't manufacture chemistry between two people. It's either there or it isn't."

Dessie nodded. "I know. But Jules seems to think there *was* chemistry between you two."

Rory sighed and drained his pint. "Yes, I knew that. It scared me. I wanted to tell her, but then I thought, maybe I could fall for her if we spent enough time together. But it didn't happen, and then I met you." He drew breath. "But I'm glad she knows. Brave of you to tell her."

Dessie sighed. "No, not brave at all. It just came out when Jules was pressing me for information. I couldn't stand lying and sneaking around anymore." She looked at her hands then back at Rory. "This doesn't mean we can now gallop around town hand in hand and show everyone we're together."

Rory frowned. "Why? What are you talking about? She knows, so where's the problem?"

"The 'problem,' as you call it, is that if we go around like a courting couple, Jules will look like a big loser, and I will be that slut who stole her sister's man—twice."

Rory nodded, looking glum. "I suppose you're right." He lifted his empty glass to the waiter at the bar, who nodded. "You want another beer, love?"

Dessie finished the last drops of her bottle of Harp. "No thanks." She got up. "I think I'd better leave. This place will be filling up soon. Don't want to start any rumours." She suddenly giggled despite herself. "Right now, the talk of the town is I'm having an affair with a sexy Englishman called Rupert."

Rory smirked. "Let's try to keep that going, then."

"Good idea."

Rory put his hand on Dessie's arm when she was about to leave. "But we can still smooch in private, can't we?"

Dessie winked. "You bet we can. But it has to be very, very private."

"No more sleazy hotels," Rory grunted.

"You have a better idea?"

"Yes, I do." He paused while the waiter put a fresh pint of beer on the table.

"Where?" Dessie asked when the coast was clear.

"My place," Rory whispered.

Dessie laughed. "Of course! We've avoided that because it's so close to Jules' place. But now that she knows..." She looked over her shoulder as a group of customers walked in. "I'm leaving. Let me know when." She winked and walked swiftly out of the pub.

CHAPTER 20

Marcus had some news when Dessie got back to Killybeg House the following day.

"There've been a lot of enquiries about the auction," he said as they walked up the winding staircase to the top floor. "And we're having a video shot here tomorrow for online issues of the major newspapers. It'll be on our website too. And," he continued, "we'll be doing a public viewing a week before the auction. We're going to open the house for three days. I have been talking to a security firm who'll be handling that. There has to be security personnel in each room to make sure nothing gets nicked, and then they'll stay on and patrol the grounds right up to the auction. The catalogue is twenty euros, and that'll be the entrance ticket, if you know what I mean."

Dessie stopped in the middle of the stairs. "Security? Is that really necessary? I mean, during the viewings, yes, but afterwards?"

Marcus rolled his eyes. "Where have you been the past week? Haven't you seen the papers? They're all full of items about the auction. The cat is out of the bag, so to speak. It has even been mentioned across Europe. This is a unique house, the contents of which are worth millions. But I bet your Richard Hourigan had something to do with that. Free publicity for the new hotel, which will be opened a year from now, or so I read."

"He's not *my* Richard Hourigan," Dessie muttered and resumed walking up the stairs. "Come on, let's get stuck in upstairs. There are eight bedrooms, all stuffed with…stuff."

She hadn't realised the enormity of the task. The bedrooms, all large, furnished with heavy mahogany, oriental rugs and thick velvet curtains, also housed an intimidating array of personal effects, such as silver-backed hairbrushes, crystal perfume spray bottles, jewellery cases (all empty), and crystal bowls for hairpins and shirt studs. The nursery also contained a large collection of dolls, all lined up on a bed, staring at Dessie with unblinking, glassy eyes. She gulped and slammed the door shut, muttering, "Spooky."

"You do realise that the catalogue has to be ready for the open house at the end of next week?" Marcus said when Dessie wanted to take a coffee break. "We have to catalogue everything up here, take photos and send the lot to be printed in Dublin. The deadline is Tuesday."

Dessie nearly burst into tears. "Shit, then we'll have to work day and night."

Marcus brushed dust off his blue sweatshirt with the Oxford cricket team logo. "Yes, my dear, we certainly do. This auction is going to be a lot bigger than we thought. We already have calls from foreign dealers. We're going to have to set up a telephone service so they can bid on the day. We even have interest from Japan."

Dessie stared at him. "Oh my God, really?"

"Yes, really. So, we'd better get a move on. Have you noted down the Victorian dressing table set?"

"Yes. I thought a hundred and fifty." She picked up a silver-backed brush from the dressing table. "Not much, but who on earth will want to brush their hair with someone else's hairbrush? Even if it's Victorian?"

"You'd be surprised."

Dessie shrugged. "I'm sure it'll sell just for the curiosity aspect." She looked around the large double bedroom, where the twin mahogany wardrobe towered above her, and the ornate bedhead and rich Oriental rug gave the room an opulent air. "What about the furniture here? Is that going to auction too?"

"No. All the bedroom furniture will be used for the hotel." Marcus peered at a picture over the chest of drawers. "What do you make of this one?"

Dessie moved over to join him. It was a small pastel portrait of a young girl, her dreamy expression, curly blonde hair, and large blue eyes oddly arresting. She studied the portrait for a moment, trying to place the muslin dress and hairstyle in the proper period. "Early English school," she said. "Very early nineteenth century, as you can tell by the slightly bouffant hairstyle that was still in fashion just before the Regency period, and the lace-trimmed dress. Enchanting."

Marcus took a measuring tape from his pocket and measured the painting. "Write this down. Fifty-five centimetres by forty-one. Price?"

Dessie tapped her pencil against her mouth. "Hmm... three to five hundred?"

"Sounds good."

And on they went, through dressing rooms and smaller bedrooms for ladies' maids and nannies, to a bathroom with a huge roll top bath and antiquated shower.

"I hope they keep this bathroom," Dessie remarked. "It's so quirky, with the mahogany toilet seat and the pull-thing to flush."

Marcus looked around. "I wouldn't think so. Too old-fashioned. I think they plan to make the smaller rooms into en-suite bathrooms so that every room has one."

"I suppose." Dessie closed the bathroom door. "But this won't be a very big hotel. I mean eight bedrooms?"

"Don't forget the servants' quarters in the attic. They'll be turned into smaller doubles. They're empty, so we don't have to bother with those. Then the gatehouse and the other out-buildings. They'll be restored and become luxury cottages. It'll be a very exclusive boutique-style hotel."

"I wish them luck," Dessie said with a derisory snort. "I can't see how a luxury hotel in the five-star price bracket will do well here in the sticks."

"I have no idea," Marcus countered. "Could be that the sporting facilities are good here. Fox hunting, pheasant shoots, hillwalking and the many excellent golf courses in the area could be big draws. Plus fly fishing in the spring, of course."

"Yeah, sure. But time will tell." She opened the door to the next bedroom. "Let's get started in here, then, so we can finish it before lunch, if that is allowed. Lunch, I mean."

"Half an hour, no more," Marcus muttered.

Dessie's phoned pinged. A message from Rory. She sneaked a look at it before she joined Marcus. How about tonight? My place @ 8. R xxx

"Put away that thing, and do try to concentrate," Marcus ordered. "We'll have to deal with our messages on our lunch break."

Dessie looked up. "Even if you get a message from Audrey?"

Marcus' eyes turned cold. "That's not very likely."

"Why? You're having problems?"

"Just to stop the inquisition—we broke up. Not that there was much to break up, actually, but there you are. I'm moving out tonight."

"Do you have to? Did she tell you to leave? Where are you going?"

"I'll be at the Bianconi Inn in town. And no, it was my own decision. Please shut up and put your phone away. We have a tight deadline."

Dessie sighed and stuck the phone back in her pocket. Her love life would have to take a back seat until after the auction.

* * *

Later that day, however, Dessie got a call she couldn't ignore. They had just tackled the nursery and catalogued the toys, Edwardian brass bed, and white wardrobe when Dessie's phone rang.

"I thought you had switched off that thing," Marcus snapped.

"I forgot." Dessie took a quick look at the caller ID. "It's from Miranda. Must be urgent. I'm taking it," she said, ignoring his glare. "Hello? Miranda? What's up?"

"It's Rory," Miranda panted. "Something has happened. I know you and he…I mean Jules told me…oh never mind. Just go there. He needs you now."

"What?" Dessie stammered, her heart racing. But Miranda had hung up.

"I have to go to Rory," Dessie said. "Something has happened. Please, Marcus, we've nearly finished for tonight anyway."

Marcus sighed. "Okay. Off you go, then. You worked hard. Sorry to have been such a slave driver. I'll go and take my stuff to the Bianconi. See you here tomorrow?"

"Of course. Bright and early. Promise." Her knees shaking, Dessie grabbed her bag and ran down the stairs and out through the door to the car. What could have happened to Rory? An accident? He said he'd be trying out a new horse. Had he been thrown off and horribly injured? She barely managed to keep the car on the road as she drove at breakneck speed to Rory's farm, coming to a screeching halt in a shower of gravel in front of the big old farmhouse. She raced to the back door she knew led to the kitchen, knowing that's where he'd be—or anyone who was helping him survive after the accident, whatever it was.

Dessie ran in through the open back door. "Rory! What…" She stopped and stared. The sight that met her eyes was not what she had expected. Rory was alive and well, sitting at the table, his head in his hands, sobbing, while Jules, her arms around him, murmured soothing words into his ear.

Jules looked up, and their eyes met.

"What happened?" Dessie gasped.

"It's his mum."

"What's she done now?"

"She died."

"Oh, dear, that's…" Dessie swallowed, fighting an irresistible urge to shout "Ding-dong, the witch is dead." Oh God. How strange. Awful for Rory, but not a huge tragedy in Dessie's estimation. She tried to adopt a sympathetic expression. "Awful," she managed.

"He's very upset," Jules said.

"Of course."

Jules got up. "I think he needs you."

"Of course." Dessie sat down on the chair beside Rory and touched his arm. "I'm here, darling. I'm so very sorry about your mum."

Rory turned his tear-stained face to Dessie and took her hand. "Thank you. I know she wasn't very nice to you, or to anyone really. But…"

"She was your mother," Dessie said. "Losing your mother is a terrible sadness."

He nodded and fished a handkerchief from his pocket.

A big Irish setter, its red coat gleaming, wandered into the kitchen and put its head on Rory's lap.

"Who's this lovely dog?" Dessie asked, stroking the soft fur.

Rory put his hand on the dog's head. "This is Nellie. She's been resting after breaking her leg six weeks ago. But she's better now. Aren't you, girl?" The dog wagged its tail and looked adoringly at Rory.

"She's lovely," Dessie said. "And she knows you're sad."

"I'll make tea," Jules said while Rory blew his nose.

"Thanks." Rory smiled shakily. "You're a brick, Jules. I didn't think you'd come here after hearing…" He shot a guilty look at Dessie.

"That's what friends do," Jules said and filled the kettle. "I'm over it anyway. I got mad when Dessie told me, but then I had a good think and realised that hey, life's too short to fall out with my sister. I forgive you. Both of you."

"How very gracious of you," Dessie snorted.

Jules laughed. "Gracious? Moi? Nah, it was Finola. She told me not to be 'so fucking precious.' Her words, not mine. So, I got a grip on myself and saw she was right. Sisters are special. Even if they go around stealing my men."

"I didn't…" Dessie started before she saw the glint in Jules' eyes. She turned back to Rory. "How did it happen? Your mum, I mean. Was it sudden?"

Rory nodded. "Yes. A massive heart attack about two hours ago. My aunt found her in her bedroom. She hadn't been feeling well and went to bed early. She must have got out of bed to call for help, but…" His eyes filled with tears again. "Poor Mam. She didn't have much luck in life. I don't know why she was so miserable to everyone, but I think most of it stemmed from her childhood. Her dad was an abusive drunk. Used to beat up both his wife and his children. She only told me this lately. I think she only married Dad to get away from all of that. I wish she had talked to me earlier. I wish I had gone to see her more often. Then we could have become closer and maybe…"

Dessie hugged him. He was heartbroken. So many regrets, so many unspoken words. "I'm sure she knows what's in your heart now. She's in a better place and not suffering anymore." She didn't know how to go on. She had hated Breda Quirke for spreading those vicious rumours all over town. It had changed Dessie's life forever. That could never be undone. Breda had also wrecked Rory's life and prevented him from having good relationships with women he loved. But that had backfired in a way Breda would never know. Dessie couldn't help smiling at the irony of it all: Rory ending up with the woman his mother had tried to destroy. What a pity she hadn't lived to see it.

Jules put three steaming mugs on the table. "Here. Tea. I'll have a mug with you, and then I'll be off."

Dessie picked up a mug. "Thanks, Jules. Tea, the most soothing remedy for nearly everything."

Rory stared at his mug. "Yes. Mam used to say…" He stopped and took a sip of tea. "No use brooding. Much to do. I have to call my sisters, start arrangements for the funeral, and see to the removal of Mam's remains to the funeral parlour." He looked at Dessie. "You'll come to the funeral?"

Dessie gave a start. The funeral? How could she go? Everyone would look at her and think… "Uh," she mumbled, absentmindedly stroking Nellie. "I…"

Jules put her hand on Dessie's. "You don't have to go. It would be an exercise in hypocrisy if you were there, pretending to mourn Breda's passing."

"She wouldn't have to pretend anything," Rory protested. "I know she has good reasons not to have liked my mother, but…" He looked at Dessie. "It would be a great help if you were there. But if you find it awkward, I understand, of course. I can see that it might look odd if you were there. But still…"

"I don't know what to do," Dessie sobbed. "Whatever I choose, it'll be wrong. I'm sorry, Rory, I know this is so hard for you, but…"

"Look, I'll be off," Jules interrupted, putting on her jacket. "I'll leave you two to sort it out. Bye, Rory. Give me a shout if there's anything I can do."

Rory nodded. "I will. Thanks for coming, Jules. I really appreciate it."

"No problem." Jules touched Dessie's shoulder. "See you,

sis." She was gone before Dessie had a chance to reply.

"Will you stay with me tonight?" Rory asked.

"Of course."

"Thank you." He picked up his phone. "I have to call my sisters. Then we'll have to make funeral arrangements. Have her…remains brought from Dungarvan to the funeral parlour here." He got up. "I'll go into my study. This could take a little time. Make yourself at home."

"Okay. I'll look around the rooms. I've never seen more than the kitchen."

"Not much to see. But feel free to roam." Rory kissed her cheek and disappeared into the study next door to the kitchen, Nellie trotting behind him.

Dessie opened the door to the corridor that led to the living and dining rooms, on either side of the front hall. The dining room was furnished with an old-fashioned set of mahogany table and eight chairs sitting on a faded Donegal rug. There was a china cabinet crammed with fine china from Belleek and a sideboard with a pair of silver candlesticks and a silver tea service. This room didn't look as if it had been used for a while, Rory preferring to take his meals in the cosy kitchen. She wandered into the living room, which was tastefully furnished with two green velvet sofas flanking the period fireplace. Here, the cream carpet was soft under Dessie's feet, and she felt like lighting the fire and settling into one of the sofas to watch a programme on the large flat-screen TV in the corner. This was an inviting room, and she guessed it was all Rory's work. He must have refurnished it after Breda left, throwing out the nineteen-fifties' furniture and cheap carpet she knew had been the style from what Miranda had told her.

A group of silver-framed photos on the mantelpiece caught Dessie's eye, and she went to have a closer look. There was a large family photo of Rory's mum and dad and four children. She spotted a tiny boy with huge eyes and a thatch of brown hair. Rory at about four. Breda and her husband smiled into the camera, their arms around each other. A happy couple with the perfect family. Dessie looked at the other boy, older than Rory, who was the image of his mother, with the same eyes, black hair, and pointy chin. That must be Brian, who died in a farm accident at the age of nineteen. The rightful heir, in other words, and his mother's darling, according to rumours. The little girls, both toddlers, had brown hair like Rory and their dad, whose good looks were duplicated in the three little faces. The other photos were of Rory with various dogs and horses, and the sisters and their families. Dessie put the photos back, thinking it was strange that she hadn't really known any of them, apart from Rory. But he had been the only one she'd been in contact with through the pony club. He was nearly ten years older and had been hero-worshipped by the horsey girls in those days. She vaguely remembered the tragedy of Brian's death and the harrowing funeral mass when she was around eight, but it hadn't really registered. The sisters looked like normal, hassled mums of small children. It would be nice to meet them.

She sat down in one of the sofas and decided to watch the evening news while she waited for Rory. Then she'd cook him something nice for dinner, if he was able to eat anything. The news had just started when her phone rang.

It was Miranda. "Hi, pet, how's Rory?"

Dessie turned down the volume. "Very sad but holding up. It was such a shock. He's talking to his sisters now, and then he'll be making arrangements for the funeral."

"Of course. How are you? Must be hard. I mean mixed feelings and all that."

"I'm glad I can be here with him now," Dessie replied, touched by the concern in Miranda's voice. "I'm going to stay with him tonight. I don't want him to be alone."

"Of course not." Miranda paused. "But what about the funeral? That'll be a huge dilemma for you."

"That's for sure," Dessie agreed. "A case of damned if I go and damned if I don't. If I sit there with Rory and his sisters, everyone will know what's going on, and if I go and sit at the back of the church, they'll wonder what the hell I'm doing there. Either way, they'll be saying I'm doing it all over again, blah, blah. Not that I care what anyone thinks, but I don't want Rory to be hurt."

"Of course not. But I've been talking to Jules, and we have come up with the perfect solution. This way, you'll be looking good, and nobody will be able to say a word against you."

"What solution?" Dessie asked.

"Just listen for a moment."

Dessie sat back and let Miranda explain. As she heard the plan, relief flooded through her like a warm wave. It was perfect.

CHAPTER 21

As expected, there was a huge turnout for Breda Quirke's funeral. The removal service the evening before had been well-attended, but nothing like the huge crowds for the funeral mass. Dessie started to shake as they were about to go into the church.

Miranda squeezed her hand. "Don't worry. It'll be fine. We're not the main event, after all."

Dessie nodded as they moved aside to let the immediate family pass. Rory gazed briefly at Dessie and smiled, mouthing a "thank you" as he escorted his sisters and his aunt into the church ahead of them. She noticed the sisters were now both blonde, but apart from that very like Rory. The aunt bore a faint resemblance to her sister, Breda, but with a softer, more kindly expression.

Jules stepped in beside Dessie. "Okay, gang. Are we ready?"

Dessie nodded. "Yes. Let's go in." And side by side, the three sisters walked up the aisle to take their seats. There was a faint communal gasp as the congregation noticed them, and Dessie could nearly feel eyes boring into her back. Her knees wobbled, and she felt suddenly unable to move. But then Jules hooked her arm through Dessie's and held her up, while they took their seats at the end of a pew just behind the family. Then the organ started, and a lone voice sang the first bars of "On Eagle's Wings," a hymn that always brought tears to Dessie's eyes.

The rest of the service was a blur as Dessie's thoughts turned to the night before. She had waited in the house while Rory was at the removal service, something they always did at Catholic funerals. The coffin was brought to the church from the funeral parlour to rest there during the night, before the funeral and burial the following day.

Rory had returned late, as there had been a wake at the local pub after the service. He'd been able to slip away, while his sisters remained to thank everyone for coming and for "giving the family such support during this hard time."

"Support, my eye," he snorted when he came back. "They're all there for free drinks. Mam didn't have many close friends, only the women in the Tidy Towns Committee and the bridge club, and they were not really bosom pals, just old biddies swapping gossip. The rest of the people there were her old classmates, who were delighted it wasn't them this time." He sighed and threw his coat on a chair in the kitchen. "I smell food. Did you cook me something, you lovely lass?"

"Sit down and I'll get it."

"Yes, ma'am." Rory sat down.

"Maybe you should have asked your sisters to stay here?" Dessie wondered, as she handed him a plate of chicken and baked potatoes. "I could easily have made more."

"No. They're here with their families. The bedrooms here are not ready for visitors. I'd have to buy new mattresses and update the linen. But they knew that. In any case, Clodagh is staying with a friend of hers who has a big house, and Orla went to a cousin in Clonmel. They'll be fine." He looked at Dessie across the steaming plate. "Will you stay here tonight? With me?"

"Of course, sweetheart."

"Thank you."

Later, in his bed, she held him tight, whispering soothing little nothings until his breathing became even and his body heavy. She lay back in the bed, staring into the darkness, wishing—hoping—the torture would soon be over.

* * *

It wasn't over by a long shot. Even though the gossips in town had been silenced by the appearance of the three sisters at the funeral, another problem appeared, a much greater one than anyone could have anticipated. It was all revealed at the lunch at the Bianconi Inn hosted by the bereaved family. Rory insisted Dessie, Jules, and Miranda join the family at their table. "You're very much family too," he said, his eyes pleading.

Dessie immediately understood. He wanted to delay any rows about the will until after the lunch and the formalities of sympathy from the rest of the congregation were over. Judging by the palpable tension between the siblings, he needed help.

"Of course, we'll sit with you," Dessie said. She held out her hand to one of the sisters. "Hello. I'm—"

"I know who you are," the woman said. "Sure, didn't we all go to the same primary school. Until you lot were sent to posh boarding schools," she added with a nasty twist to her mouth.

"Yeah, but you weren't that blonde then," Jules cut in. "You must be Clodagh. I'm Jules, the rowdy one."

Clodagh nodded. "Hello."

"I'm Orla," the other sister said and held out her hand. "I haven't been home for like a hundred years, so I don't blame you for not recognising me." She turned to a stocky man behind her. "This is my husband, Fintan." She pointed at a tall, balding man coming toward them carrying a pint.

"That's Clodagh's husband. His name's Pat, and he's just lost his job. He was working for a construction company that went broke. Took them a while after the crash, but they finally managed it. Just when things are picking up again," she added, her voice dripping with schadenfreude. Although both sisters bore a startling resemblance to Rory, neither of them had his sweetness of expression or warmth.

Murmuring polite platitudes, they sat down at the table, picking at the food, the air practically crackling with tension. Except for a brief word here and there, nobody mentioned Breda with any sorrow, and Dessie deduced that the sisters had hated their mother with a passion.

"Mam got a nice send-off," Clodagh said over the chocolate pudding.

"She had a lot of friends," Rory said. "She was great at running things."

"Yes," Orla muttered. "I'll give her that."

Rory put down his spoon. "Look, I've had enough of this. Mam might not have been the cuddliest of mothers, but she was hard-working and loyal. Okay, so she was very bossy and wanted to run the farm her way. But then she finally gave in and handed it all over to me. We were actually on very friendly terms before she moved to live with Auntie Olive."

Olive nodded. "That's true, Rory. Breda softened a lot after that. Could have been her heart problem or old age, but she was much more gentle and caring during the past year. We were good friends. I'm going to miss her a great deal."

"I'm sorry I didn't go to see her," Orla said. "But I didn't know about her change of heart. Pity."

"She'd be happy to know about us," Clodagh said. "I mean, Pat and me and the kids. We're moving back home. Back to the farm. We'll help you run it, Rory. I was going to keep it as a surprise, but I thought it would cheer you up to hear it right now."

The colour drained from Rory's face. "What? You're…?"

Clodagh beamed at him. "I knew you'd be over the moon. Yes, you heard right. Pat and I are coming home. I mean, we own a third of the farm now, don't we? Unless Mam made a will."

Rory looked at his aunt. "Did she?"

"Not as far as I know," Olive said. "She said she wanted everything to be shared equally."

"But Clodagh didn't tell you everything," Orla interrupted. "I've decided to let her run the farm, as long as she shares some of the income with me. Say hi to your new boss, Rory."

"Jesus," Rory whispered, staring at Clodagh.

She grinned. "Best news all day, eh? Pat and I will shake things up at the old place. We have some great plans. Pat's going to build an extension at the back so we can have two new bedrooms and a bathroom. And the kids will love living on a farm. I've promised them they can rear pigs and goats. And I'm getting ponies for them both. They can't wait."

Speechless, Rory kept staring at his sisters. He turned to Dessie, and they looked at each other in the mutual knowledge that everything had suddenly changed. And not for the better.

* * *

"Holy shit, what a fucking mess," Finola said. They were in Jules' conservatory the following evening sharing a bottle of wine and a pizza.

"I know," Dessie sighed. "Just when we thought everything was beginning to sort itself out. I was even planning to move in with Rory after the auction."

Finola shook her head. "Poor Rory. He really has no luck with women. Except with you, of course, Dessie. I meant the women in his family."

Jules helped herself to another slice of pizza. "It's a disaster for him. He loves the farm. He was just starting to make money with those two brood mares. Two of their offspring won some big races last year. Hard work, but it's finally paying off."

"He told me he was thinking of switching to horses full-time," Dessie remarked. "He's not really fond of cattle and thinks beef production harms the environment."

"And he was going to lease more land to Miranda's organic vegetable farm," Jules cut in. "I bet Clodagh will say no to that."

"Well, she'll have to wait until the probate has been sorted," Finola said. "But that's just a formality." She shook her head in disbelief. "Rory will only own a third of the farm after that. Unbelievable. It's as if Breda is getting her revenge from beyond the grave. Creepy."

Jules poured herself more wine. "But I wonder if Clodagh really knows the reality of living on a farm?"

"She grew up here," Finola argued.

"Yes, but she's been living in Dublin for over fifteen years," Jules said. "I bet she's forgotten the cold and rain and mud. Plus, two nearly teenage kids who know nothing about country living. I bet they won't be getting up at dawn to muck out those ponies she's promised them. Or take to living far away from town and having to be driven to every activity. Not to mention that lame husband of hers. He's a Dubliner." Jules got up. "We need more wine. And I have some lovely goat's cheese from Miranda's farm shop. Won't be a tick."

Finola looked at Dessie. "So," she said. "Things have been happening while I've been away, I gather."

Dessie swallowed her last piece of pizza. "Yes, but I'm sure I don't have to tell you anything."

"No." Finola paused. "I was sad for Jules that she and Rory didn't work out. They seemed so good together. Then you stepped in, and he turned into a randy teenager. I can see why. You're sexy as hell. I'm only glad you weren't around when Colin was in the neighbourhood."

"What do you mean?" Dessie snapped. "I don't go around—"

"I know. Of course not. That was my insecurities talking. You're scary stuff for women like me. I know you and Rory just have that special something, though. Jules saw that too, eventually. But now, with all this going on, you're the one with the problem. In any case, if this hadn't happened, what were you planning to do? Give up your career and move back here? Seems like a big step backwards, if you don't mind my saying so."

Dessie laughed. "I don't mind. But I have a feeling you'd say it anyway, even if I did mind."

"You bet I would. I'm a nosy old reporter. Can't stop myself asking questions."

"Just ignore her," Jules said from the door. "She'd get secrets from an oyster. Before you know it, you'll have told her your life story, including your past sins, your sexual fantasies, and your dark thoughts."

Finola's eyes widened in mock innocence. "I don't know what you mean, Jules. I was just making conversation."

"That's how she does it." Jules put a bottle and a plate with cheese and crackers on the table. "But I've been thinking…"

"Yes?" Dessie and Finola said in unison.

"There might be a way to turn Clodagh's country dream into a nightmare that will send her screaming back to the city."

Finola brightened. "An evil plan? I love evil plans. Especially if they're sneaky as well."

Jules let out an evil cackle. "This one's the mother of all sneakiness."

They all jumped at the sound of the back door opening with a crash. Seconds later, Rory stood at the door of the conservatory, breathing hard, his eyes wild and his hair ruffled by the wind. Nellie padded in behind him and sat down at his side.

"I was looking for you," Rory said to Dessie. "I have something to tell you." His eyes shifted to Jules and Finola. "Hi. Sorry for bursting in like this. But—"

"We know," Finola said. "We were just talking about what's going on. And we thought…we kind of have a plan…"

"I don't need a plan," Rory snapped. "I have it all worked out. But I need legal help to sort some stuff out."

"What are you going to do?" Finola asked.

"I'm not going to tell you. I don't want it on the front page of The Irish Times tomorrow."

"I wasn't asking as a journalist," Finola protested, looking hurt.

"Maybe not. But I don't want to tell anyone about this until it's all set to go."

"Not even me?" Dessie asked.

Rory pushed his hand through his hair. "No…well, yeah. I don't know. Can I have a word in private?"

Dessie got up. "Let's talk in the kitchen."

"Okay. Oh, and Jules? I need you to take my hunter while I'm away. I'll get one of the lads to bring him over tomorrow. He's completely sound now, so you can hunt him, or let that English guy ride him. Seems like he knows his way around horses."

"No problem," Jules replied. "Marcus will be delighted to hunt that terrific horse."

"Great, thanks. Bye, girls," Rory said over his shoulder as he followed Dessie out. "Sorry I interrupted your evening."

Dessie waited for Rory in the cloakroom outside the kitchen. "We can talk here. What was it you wanted to explain?"

Rory took her hands. "Dessie, please don't take this the wrong way. I love you. Don't ever forget that."

She nodded. "Go on. There's a 'but' coming, right?"

He squeezed her hands. "Yes. I think we should take a break. I don't want you to be involved in things that might get ugly."

"What do you mean?" Dessie pulled away. "Take a break? But I want to be with you. Support you. Stand by you when you face the…whatever you're up against."

Rory's face turned to stone. "No. I must do this on my own. I've been bossed around by women all my life. It's time I coped on my own."

"And I'm one of them? One of those bossy women?" A red-hot wave of anger rose in Dessie's chest. "You know, it took a lot of guts to walk up the aisle this morning. And I didn't particularly enjoy sitting at the luncheon table with your snippy sisters. But I did it for you."

Rory sighed. "I know. And I appreciated that. But look, you've been fighting for your independence for a long time. You weren't even sure whether you wanted to move in with me or go back to London and your career. That was a huge struggle for you. Now, I'm fighting to do something life-changing. It's a watershed moment for me. I have plans—big plans—that I know you'll be very happy about. But I can't reveal them until it's all set in motion." He drew breath and put his hands on her shoulders. "I'm going away. I can't tell you where, or when I'll be back. But when it's all in the bag, so to speak, I'll let you know."

Speechless, Dessie stared at him. "You're going away? But what about the farm, the horses?"

"That's all taken care of. I've hired extra staff and Jules will take my hunter."

"What about Nellie?" Dessie looked at the dog standing at Rory's side as if she were part of his shadow.

"She's coming with me." He kissed her forehead. "Bye, sweetheart. Good luck with the auction. I'll be in touch. Keep the faith."

Before Dessie had a chance to say anything—even goodbye—he was gone, the door swinging in the wind, letting in a cold blast of air.

Dessie wobbled across the kitchen and back into the conservatory.

Jules looked up as she entered. "Dessie? You're as white as a sheet. What happened?"

Dessie stared blindly at her. "Is there any more wine?"

CHAPTER 22

After Rory's dramatic exit, Dessie threw herself into the work of the final days before the auction. There was much to do and little time to get it all done, but she was happy to have something to take her mind off her heartache. She worked late into the night, proofreading the catalogue, setting up the rooms before the viewings, and answering calls from the press. The video had attracted a lot of attention, and the major newspapers called the house a "time capsule" the likes of which had never been seen before.

The public viewings were a huge success, with queues snaking all the way down the avenue to the entrance gates. Most of the visitors had to wait more than an hour, as only small groups were let in every half hour. Dessie was on duty full-time, swearing she didn't mind spending all day at the viewings. She was only too happy to have little time to brood. Marcus was delighted, as this gave him a chance to take time off for hunting.

"Jules gave me Rory's horse," he announced. "Wonderful animal. Such a treat to hunt in this fabulous countryside."

Dessie would normally have started one of her usual anti-hunting rants, but she found she couldn't be bothered. She just shrugged and threw herself back into the last frenzied days. The conference room at the Bianconi Inn had to be prepared, telephone lines set up, all the major pieces transported from the house to the hotel, and security organised for the more valuable lots.

There were rumours flying around about Rory that Dessie tried her best to ignore. Some of it sounded too far-fetched to be true, in any case. Jules filled her in on the basic facts that she had heard from Clodagh, who had moved into the farmhouse as soon as Rory left.

"Does she know where he went?" Dessie asked when she called in for late supper the evening before the auction.

"No. No idea. She's annoyed he just took off like that without telling her where he was going."

"I thought she'd be delighted. Now she can do what she wants with the farm."

"Not quite. Probate takes a month or so. She seems certain it'll work out her way in the end. But…" Jules paused. "I wonder what Rory is up to. I have this odd feeling he'll be pulling the carpet from under them very soon."

Dessie shrugged. "Whatever he's planning, he didn't share it with me."

"I believe you. I think he has some kind of agenda, and he wants to be left alone while he sorts everything out."

Clodagh didn't believe Dessie, however, which she didn't hesitate to say during a venom-laced phone call around midnight. "I don't know what the feck he's up to, or where he is," she hissed. "He just took that jeep and trailer with one of the mares and said he was bringing it to the sales in Dublin. I haven't heard from him since. But you know where he is, so don't try to deny it. Whatever it is the two of you are cooking up, it won't work. Orla and I are the main owners of this farm, and we have great plans for it. You can tell that miserable shit he won't be able to crawl back here. I've dumped all his belongings in the barn and changed the locks."

"Uh, is that legal?" Dessie asked when Clodagh paused for breath.

"That's none of your business. Keep your nose out of our affairs, if you know what's good for you."

"Charming," Dessie muttered and hung up. She turned the phone to flight mode, pulled up the duvet and tried to go to sleep. But her thoughts kept turning back to Rory. Where was he? What was he doing? Why had he left so suddenly? And why had there been no word from him since he left? It had only been a few days, but it felt like months. She longed to see him again, to feel his arms around her, to breathe in his special smell, to hear his deep voice. It was as if a part of her had been ripped away, leaving her cold and miserable and without an anchor. Was he ever coming back? She closed her burning eyes and tried to sleep. The auction was only a day away. She'd have plenty of time to worry after that.

* * *

Afterwards, Dessie could hardly remember the auction— or what she saw of it standing at the back. The only thing that stood out was Marcus' performance as auctioneer. Spellbound, she watched him call out the lots and heard his voice, like a Gregorian chant, starting off the bidding and keeping it going up and up, not missing a nod or a lifted finger, until he saw it would go no higher. She didn't think she'd ever master that skill.

At the end of the day, most of the items went for a lot more than the starting price, fetching, in all, close to a million euros. It was a sensation. A huge victory for Smythe's. And for Dessie.

Marcus beamed at her as they celebrated afterwards with a glass of champagne in the plush bar of the hotel. He touched her glass with his. "Cheers, Dessie. You did a jolly good job. Dad was impressed. Pity he couldn't be here, but he came down with a nasty bug just before he was about to travel."

"I'm sorry to hear that."

"I didn't mind him not being here, breathing down my neck." Marcus grinned. "But after my glowing report, he said he wants to see you when you come back. But not until after the holidays. We close down until the new year, but then there are a lot of new auctions to get your teeth into."

"Sounds great. Especially the bit about taking a break. I feel a little burnt out."

"I can imagine. I say, did you see Richard Hourigan at the auction?"

"No."

"He was sitting in the middle of the room somewhere." Marcus looked around the crowded bar. "I thought he'd be here, celebrating."

"Maybe he went to celebrate somewhere else?"

Marcus shrugged. "No idea. Never mind. Not a very pleasant chap anyway."

"He must be pleased with the result of the auction." Dessie finished the last drops in her glass.

"How about another glass?" Marcus asked, lifting the bottle from the cooler.

Dessie pushed her glass away. "No thanks. Can't get totally pissed. With my luck, I'm bound to be caught by the Guards. It's Friday night. They're always out there trying to catch drunk drivers. But you go ahead and get as drunk as a skunk if you want."

"Absolutely," Marcus said with feeling. "I need to drown my sorrows."

"You have sorrows?" Dessie asked, looking at Marcus' handsome face which didn't show the slightest sign of sorrow. "Still smarting after the break-up with Audrey?"

Marcus shook his head. "No. Not smarting at all. A clean break was the best thing. I was barking up the wrong girl, which I realised very quickly." He peered at her. "You, on the other hand, look a little sad around the gills."

"Gills? I'm not a fish."

"No, but you're pale and drawn. A little tiff with the boyfriend?"

Dessie fixed him with a cold stare. "I don't appreciate your condescending tone."

Marcus held up his hands. "Okay, okay, I get it. Gosh, you Broadbent sisters are a tough bunch to handle. But I admire your chutzpah."

"How do you think we survived in this country all these years?"

"I'm beginning to see the picture." Marcus slid from the barstool. "How about getting a table and some food? I believe the cuisine here is excellent."

"Good idea, old chap." In her eagerness, Dessie nearly toppled from her stool, but a strong male hand under her elbow stopped her fall. She turned to the man. "Thank you." Then she saw who it was. "Richard. Eh, hello."

"Hello, Dessie. And…" He nodded at Marcus.

Marcus smiled politely. "Marcus Smythe. Good evening. I trust you're well? And quite pleased with the auction?"

"Very pleased," Richard replied. "I just came in to say thank you. I'll be staying in the gatehouse for a few days, as the housekeeper informed me that the master bedroom is free."

"That's right," Marcus replied. "I've moved into the hotel. But I won't be staying on for Christmas. Dessie's sister Jules has offered me accommodation over the holidays."

"What?" Her mouth open, Dessie looked from one to the other in shock. "Richard…I had no idea. Audrey didn't tell me. And Marcus? You're staying for Christmas? With Jules?" She put her hand to her forehead. "I'm getting a headache."

"Food," Marcus declared and pulled at Dessie's arm. "I see a table over there. Sorry we can't invite you, old man, but it's a table for two."

"Of course," Richard said. He touched Dessie's shoulder. "I'll see you later, Dessie. At the gatehouse?"

Before she had a chance to reply, Richard had pushed through the crowd and disappeared. "Was he really here?" she mumbled. "Or have I drifted into some kind of twilight zone?"

Marcus pulled her along to their table. "Sit. You need food."

Dessie flopped down on the chair. "What was that about you moving in with Jules?" she asked as she took the menu from a waiter who had appeared as if conjured up by Marcus.

Marcus opened his menu. "Not 'moving in' as such. She offered me a room in that big old house of hers over Christmas. You see, the hunting here on Boxing Day and the days afterwards is legendary. I don't want to miss it. And as I'm riding Rory's horse while he's away in England, she asked if I'd help her out with the other horses during the holidays. She'll be flat out with the hirelings. She's providing horses for a huge number of visitors from overseas. Her stable lad will be on holiday, so there's the cleaning and feeding after a day's hunting, not to mention the mucking out of around eight horses. Tough work, but if she can do it, so can I." He winked. "But I don't mind telling you that your sister is one hell of a woman. A wonderful rider. She knows about horse-flesh. I've never seen such magnificent hunters."

"Oh." Dessie frowned. "I see. But…hang on. What was that about Rory? Did you say he's…in England?"

"I think I'll have the Thai chicken curry," Marcus muttered from behind the menu. "What about you?"

Dessie pulled away his menu. "Answer my question. Is Rory in England?"

Marcus nodded. "Yes. Thought you knew. Give me back the menu."

"I didn't know. How did you hear this?"

"Jules." Marcus grabbed the menu back.

"Jules knows?"

"Yes. She only just found out. I think he e-mailed her. Something to do with his horse."

"What's he doing there?"

Marcus shrugged. "Haven't a clue. Visiting friends? Selling horses? Shopping in Bond Street?"

Dessie stared at him, feeling tears well up. Rory went to England without telling her. What was he up to? Had he found someone else? An English girl?

"Stop thinking the worst," Marcus ordered. "I'm sure he'll be in touch soon. Or you could e-mail him or something."

"He told me not to contact him and that he'd let me know when…when everything was in place."

Marcus nodded. "There you go, then. He'll come back when he's ready. If that's what he said, you should not contact him."

"Why not?"

"Not a good move to look needy, dear girl. You know the old saying: 'Leave them alone, they will come home, wagging their tails behind them.'"

"That's a nursery rhyme."

"Never were truer words spoken by a nursery rhyme. Come on, forget about him. What do you want to eat?"

"Nothing," Dessie whispered, her chin wobbling. She just wanted to crawl into bed and cry.

"Come on, old fruit, chin up. I thought you said you Anglo-Irish women had chutzpah."

"I think I lost it."

"You need food. And I need wine. Lots of wine. You can have a glass without going over the limit." Marcus waved at a waiter. "We'll both have the Thai chicken curry. And a bottle of the Beaujolais, which you might bring us straight away."

When the wine had been opened and poured, Marcus held up his glass. "What shall we drink to?"

Dessie shrugged. "Don't know. I've nothing much to cheer about."

"To our amazing luck in love?"

Despite her worries, Dessie couldn't help giggling. She

clinked glasses with Marcus. "I'll drink to that. Nice to dine with a fellow loser."

"What's wrong with us, do you think?" Marcus asked as they tucked into the steaming plates of hot curry. "I must admit to being puzzled. I mean, here we are, both stunning, intelligent, and successful. Yet we can't make anyone fall for us. Not even each other."

"Aura," Dessie said. "I've always thought I had a problem with mine. Maybe you do too? We probably have the wrong ones."

"What can we do about that, then? Is there a workshop where we could go and have our auras fixed? Or maybe buy new ones?"

"I think we're stuck with the ones we have." Dessie munched on a coriander leaf while she studied Marcus. He was handsome in that clean-cut British way, with a tall, fit body, great charm and slightly wacky sense of humour. Why was he so unlucky in love? "We're just bad at picking the right partners," she said after a moment's deliberation. "But I'm sure you'll find someone who'll be perfect for you one day."

"Will it take long? I'm tired of waiting."

"She might be right under your nose."

Marcus stared at her. "What? You mean—?"

"No." Dessie laughed. "Not me. Could be someone you meet regularly and you like a lot, but you haven't got the spark yet. Someone with whom you have a lot in common."

"Oh." He looked thoughtful. "I see...hmmm. Yes... maybe..."

"Aha!" Dessie pointed at him with her fork. "You just realised who it could be. And now you're all pink and mushy."

Marcus squirmed. "Oh, please. Don't go all Mills and Boon on me."

Dessie suddenly had a brainwave. "Jules!" she chortled. "It's Jules, isn't it? You're very drawn to her. Riding, hunting, horses...oh my God, how perfect!"

Marcus' face turned an interesting shade of pink. "I don't know what you mean."

"Yes you do."

"Please. Do shut up."

Dessie smirked. "My lips are sealed. I won't say another word."

"Thank you."

"But I'm still loving it. I mean, you and Jules…" Dessie stopped when Marcus glared at her. "Okay, okay. I'll stop. I want to get home and go to bed anyway." She dug in her bag for her credit card. "Ask for the bill, will you? We'll split it."

Marcus put his hand on hers. "Dinner's on me. Just to thank you for all your hard work."

"Oh. Okay. Thank you. But I enjoyed it." Dessie got up. "I suppose I'll see you at Jules' sometime?"

"When I'm not at the stables. But…" He peered at her over his plate of curry. "Are you going to be all right? I mean with that cad staying in the same house?"

"I'll be fine," Dessie said with pretend bravado. "Audrey will protect me."

Marcus laughed. "In that case, I'm not worried. That is one scary woman."

But when Dessie got to the gatehouse, she met Audrey carrying a suitcase, a meowing Cat under her arm. "I wish you luck staying with that pile of shit," she snarled. "I'm moving out."

CHAPTER 23

Dessie stood rooted to the spot, watching Audrey throw her bag into her car and place Cat carefully on the back seat. "Where are you going?"

"Miranda's. She offered me a bed for the night. In any case, she needs a bit of help with the boys now that Aiden's in college. She and Jerry want to go away for a break before the Christmas holidays. You could stay there too. The guest room has two beds."

"What happened with…?" Dessie jerked her head toward the house.

"He tried to hit on me. Didn't take no for an answer. Said he owns the house and I owed him. American men, huh? Think they're God's gift to women."

"Holy shit."

"Hey, come with me," Audrey called from the car. "You don't want to be alone with that creep."

"I'm not afraid of him."

"Well, whatever. I'm off. You know where to go if you need a bed." Audrey started the car and drove off.

Dessie sighed and walked to the front door. She didn't quite know why, but she felt an irresistible urge to confront Richard. Maybe she could finally get that closure she needed? But when she walked in, the house was in darkness. She could hear music from the master bedroom upstairs.

Richard must be in bed either watching TV or listening to the radio. Relieved, Dessie tiptoed to her bedroom and closed the door, turning the key in the lock. She didn't want any surprise visitors.

As she undressed, her thoughts turned to Rory. He had made her promise not to contact him until he came back. She had thought he was in Dublin trying to get Orla on his side and maybe consulting a solicitor about the will. But now he was in England doing—what? In bed, she grabbed her phone. What harm could a text message do? She quickly typed a short message before she changed her mind. What are u doing in England? I miss you. I love you. I can't stand this much longer. With tears running down her cheeks, she pressed "send," threw the phone into her bag and pulled the covers over her head. He wasn't going to reply, but she had at least told him how she felt.

Exhausted, she closed her eyes and finally drifted off to sleep. Half an hour later, her phone pinged. Dessie's eyes flew open. She turned on the light and searched for her phone. A text message from Rory. Sobbing, she read it: I'm on my way back. Trust me and hang in there. R x

Dessie let out a long sigh. It was okay. He would come back to her. Eventually. All she had to do was wait—and figure out what to do about her career.

* * *

After a restless night, Dessie woke up to a door banging down the corridor. She sat up. Who was that? Richard already up? She turned on the light and checked the time. Seven thirty. Saturday morning. She had to get up and go up to the house. Then she remembered the auction and the evening with Marcus. It was all over and she had a whole two weeks off. But she had to leave the gatehouse and either go back to London or stay in Cloughmichael over Christmas. Miranda had said something about Christmas dinner and the rest of the holidays. Trying to get everything sorted in her head, Dessie got up, showered, and dressed. While she packed, she could hear Richard moving around in the kitchen, banging cupboard doors and turning on the kettle. He was having his breakfast. The perfect time to have that all-important talk before they parted company forever.

Her heart beating, and her stomach contracting, Dessie walked into the kitchen, where she found Richard at the table eating bacon, eggs, and toast while listening to the early morning news on the radio.

He looked up. "Good morning. Up early as well?"

Dessie hesitated by the door. "Yeah, well, I have to get going. All my work is done, so I'm leaving."

"Going where?" Ricard enquired, a strange look in his eyes.

"Uh, I'm going to stay with my sister Miranda. I'm spending Christmas with her and her family."

"I see." He smirked. "But not quite yet, right?"

Dessie stiffened. "What do you mean?"

"Have you looked outside?"

"No…I mean, why?" Dessie walked to the window, pulled the curtain and gasped. "Oh my God! Snow! It must have snowed all night." She stared at the white world outside in disbelief.

Richard nodded. "That's right, sweetie. Nobody is going anywhere for quite some time."

"But…how? I never heard that snow was forecast for the weekend. I thought they said it would snow heavily in the north, but stay quite mild down here."

"Well," Richard drawled and stretched out his legs. "It looks like they were wrong, doesn't it?"

"Shit," Dessie moaned. "Shit, shit, shit!"

"Yeah, well, we're all right here, aren't we?"

Dessie twirled around. "No we're not! I don't want to stay one more second in the same house as you."

"I don't think you have much of a choice, baby."

"I can't believe it," Dessie groaned, pacing around the kitchen. "This is just the pits." She peered out the window again. Maybe it wasn't as bad as he pretended? But she realised there was at least four inches of snow on the ground already and it was still coming down. All the roads would be blocked. Could she walk? It was a good ten kilometres to town and Miranda's house, which would take two hours on foot in normal conditions. Jules was about the same distance in the other direction, down a narrow track. She wasn't even sure she would be able to find it in this weather. She was truly stuck. The only vehicle that could cope would be a four-by-four. Dessie suddenly had an idea. Jules. She had an old jeep she used for pulling the trailer for hunting. Dessie took her mobile from her pocket and punched in Jules' number. Her voicemail kicked in straight away. Shit. She must be busy looking after the horses. Dessie quickly left a brief message after the beep. "Hi, Jules. Stuck in the gatehouse. Need help to get out. Please come as soon as you can." Dessie drew breath. "She'll be here soon," she said to Richard.

"Come on," Richard said. "Relax. Have some breakfast. There's fresh bread, eggs, and bacon. And I just made a pot of tea."

"I'm not hungry."

"Don't be silly. Of course you are. Sit down, willya? I'm not going to eat you."

Dessie sighed and pushed back her hair. He was right. She should calm down and have something to eat. She glanced at him. Was he really the kind of man who'd take advantage of the situation? She sneaked a look at him while he ate his bacon. Why had she found him so attractive all those years ago? With his dark hair, blue eyes, and boyish face, he was good-looking in a superficial way, but his mouth was slack and his eyes lacked warmth and any real empathy.

"I'm not going to attack you, if that's what you're worried about," Richard said, as if reading her mind.

Dessie stared at him. "That's not what Audrey said last night."

Richard raised his eyebrows. "What? Oh that. I was a little drunk, to be honest. And there she was, wearing a short skirt and those boots. What's a guy to do?"

"How old are you, fifteen? Surely you can keep your hands off a woman even if she's wearing a short skirt."

"Dressed like that, she looked like she was asking for it."

Dessie rolled her eyes. "To you, yes. But of course, you wouldn't understand the concept of fashion." Suddenly, like red-hot lava, all her pent-up anger welled up. She wanted to hit him hard. She took a deep breath and charged. "You know what, Richard? You're the kind of man who turns women *off* sex, not *on*. The kind of man who thinks we're all 'asking for it,' who thinks with his dick and not with his brain. Which is of course because you haven't got one." Dessie stared at Richard's crotch. "It's all down there, isn't it? You're that 'pussy-grabbing' guy that's so in the news right now, from whom we run away. You can buy yourself some bimbo or force yourself on an innocent young girl like you did with me, but in the end, nobody likes you. We all spit on you. We despise you. You're not a real man, just a miserable little wimp."

Richard turned white. "What do you mean? I didn't force myself on you. It wasn't exactly rape, darling. You were very willing."

Dessie felt herself go cold. "Willing? You seduced me. You made me believe…" She stopped. "I really don't want to go there. All I want to say is that it ruined something for me. It changed my life. Made me a different person."

Richard's eyes widened. "I didn't…knock you up, did I? Is there a baby out there I should know about?"

"No, there isn't," Dessie snarled. "Thank God." Exhausted

after her rant, she sank down on a chair. She wanted to walk out, but the anger kept her all fired up. She glared at him. "What you did to me that summer changed my life. Not the sex, but you dumping me like that. It triggered a series of events that forced me to leave my home town. It also made my life take a whole new direction, which was a good thing, I suppose. But it was a long, hard road. I'm okay now, and I'm strong and independent. Men like you have no power over me."

"What a brave little speech." Richard rose from his chair and walked toward her. "All that fire makes you suddenly very attractive." He touched her cheek. "We're all alone here in this cosy house…"

Dessie jumped up and backed away, grabbing the bread knife from the counter. "Don't come near me, you big shite, or…"

"Or what?" Richard folded his arms and studied her in a way that made her squirm. It was as if he were undressing her with his eyes. "Back then, you were a delicious young girl in a summer dress, with stars in your eyes. Rather hard to resist, I have to say. But now…" He stepped closer, so close she could feel his breath on her face. He ran his hand down her arm. "Now, you're a woman. With that black hair, those green eyes, and the face and the figure…"

Suddenly weak with fear, Dessie closed her eyes and let the bread knife fall to the floor with a clatter. Then she heard it. A faint rumble at first, growing louder and louder, until it turned into a wonderfully familiar sound. Flooded with relief, she was at last able to move. "Jules," she breathed. "Thank God. She's here."

Strong headlights shone in through the kitchen window and the jeep drew up with a screech outside. Dessie flew to the door and flung it open, finding not Jules but Rory, covered in a dusting of snow. Sobbing, she fell into his arms. "You're here. Oh God, please tell me it's not a dream."

"It's real. It's me. I'm back." He hugged her tight, so tight the wet snow from his jacket soaked into her sweater.

Richard stared at them. "What the…?"

"I might ask the same question. What's going on here?" Rory demanded. "Who's this guy, Dessie, and what's he doing here?"

Richard drew himself up to his full height. "I'm Richard Hourigan, the owner of Killybeg House. Who the fuck are you?"

"Rory Quirke. I live nearby. I'm Dessie's fiancé, and I've come to get her out of here and to her sister's house."

Richard stepped away. "Be my guest. I'll be glad to get rid of these hysterical women."

"Fiancé?" Dessie laughed. "What do you mean? Where's the ring?"

"We'll get one as soon as the snow stops," Rory replied, kissing the top of her head. "If you're ready, we'll get out of here. Jules is expecting us. I think she's making breakfast if she's finished with the horses. I promised to get Marcus from the hotel later, so he can give her a hand. But I wanted to get you first."

"I've never been readier," Dessie sang and pulled Rory through the kitchen. "My suitcase is all packed. Come on, let's get it and go."

Rory needed no further encouragement. It didn't take them long to get Dessie's belongings and load them all into the jeep. With a sigh of relief, Dessie banged the door shut on Richard's sour face and got into the jeep beside Rory. "Come on, let's go!" She kissed his cheek. "Thank you for rescuing me, even if your shining armour is all wet." She paused. "And yes, I will."

Rory looked at her with tenderness. "Will what, sweetheart?"

"Marry you, of course. Whenever, however, wherever. I'll give up my job in London and look for something around here. Won't be too hard, there are plenty of auctioneering firms in Kilkenny, and—" She jumped as a wet tongue licked her face. Turning, she discovered Nellie in the back seat. "Hi, Nellie," she squealed and rubbed the red fur. "Did you hear that? I'm giving up my job for your master."

Rory silenced her with a kiss. "You won't have to do that. We'll be living in England." He started the engine.

"What are you talking about?" Dessie shouted above the rumble of the engine.

Rory winked. "Can't tell you quite yet. But stay tuned for some startling news."

The jeep wobbled over ice and snow down the drive. Dessie stared into the whirling white mass illuminated by the headlights, holding on to her seat. Where were they going from here? She turned and looked at Rory's determined face, his strong hands on the wheel. It didn't matter. As long as they were together, she'd go anywhere.

CHAPTER 24

He revealed his plan over hot chocolate in Jules' messy kitchen.

Dessie warmed her hands on her mug, sitting as close to the AGA stove as she could while Nellie nuzzled her knee.

Rory sat down in the other chair. "Listen to me," he started. "It'll seem completely nuts, but it's what I want to do. A clean break is the best in this situation. A new start for us both, on equal terms."

Dessie nodded, her heart racing. The sparkle in his eyes and his bright smile meant this would be something new and exciting. "I'm listening."

"I'm selling the farm. I mean, the farm will be sold." He held up his hand when Dessie started to protest. "Don't say anything until I've finished." He took a deep breath. "Yes, the farm is going. I have managed to persuade Orla that this is the way to go. We'll get seven million for it, if not more. Four hundred acres of the best land in the country. This isn't called the Golden Vale for nothing. With Orla on my side, Clodagh is forced by law to agree to the sale. I don't think she's that into farming anyway. I just saw her, and the kids are kicking up a fuss. No proper Wi-Fi and miles to walk to the school bus every morning, rain or shine. Not what city kids dream of. And that's only the start of country living." He snorted a laugh. "I could get the farm back if I wanted just by waiting for a while. Wouldn't take long. But I don't want to. Then they'd still own more than me. In any case, Orla is all for selling. She needs the money, and so does Clodagh, if she'd only admit it." Rory finished his chocolate and put the mug on the kitchen table.

Dessie nodded. "Okay. So you're selling the farm. A big wrench, but I see that you're determined to do this. What next? England? What's that all about?"

"I went over there with one of my horses that was sold to a stud near Cheltenham. I spent a week there, talking to people in the business. I also went to see a small stud farm that's for sale. Perfect place. Two hundred acres. Old house that needs a bit of an update, but very nice. You'll love it. The stud part has only just been refurbished. There are twenty stables, a foaling box with CCTV, a horse walker, and an arena. But that's all my side of things."

"But that's in Gloucestershire. The Cotswolds, right?"

"Yup. Not too far from London, so you could commute. Or we could buy a small flat and you could…"

Dessie dropped her mug, making Nellie yelp. "Are you serious? This sounds like some weird dream. Please tell me I'm not dreaming." She patted Nellie. "Sorry, darling, did I scare you?"

"You're not dreaming. You and me and Nellie are moving to England. And I get to work with horses, which has always been my dream. No more cows for me."

"And I can keep my job and you. And Nellie." Dessie laughed and threw herself at Rory. She kissed his face, his ears, his hair, and finally tumbled him onto the floor just as Jules walked in, accompanied by her motley crew of dogs, who started to bark and join in the fun.

"Hey!" Jules shouted. "What the hell's going on here? Are you having an orgy in my kitchen?"

Rory got up, pulling Dessie with him. "Yes. We're celebrating. We're moving to England. I'm finally cutting the apron strings and getting away from all those women."

Jules laughed and looked at Dessie. "Only to get into the clutches of another one, I see."

"But I'm going to let Rory be the boss," Dessie protested, brushing dog hair from her jeans. "And we're going to live in the Cotswolds, so I'll have to dress like one of those home counties women and learn to say 'raaather' and 'jolly good sheuw.'"

Jules laughed. "You can take lessons from Marcus. He has the fruity accent down to a T. Hey, Rory, go and get Mr Poshface for me. He can't wait to get out of the Inn. They've run out of bacon, and the heating broke down. I'm going to get him to shovel snow in the yard. That should warm him up no end. Where are you two staying?"

Rory looked at Dessie. "I'm staying with my friend Fergal. But he only has a small room with a single bed. Can you stay with Jules?"

Jules squirmed. "Er…no…I only just made up Marcus' room. The other bedrooms don't even have beds, except for Tony's, but he's coming home tonight for the holidays, if the trains are still running."

Dessie sighed and sat down on the chair she had just vacated. "I can't go back to the gatehouse and that creep, Richard. But I can bunk in with Audrey at Miranda's."

Jules took off her wet jacket and threw it on a chair. "Okay. Sounds like a good plan. Rory can drop you off there on his way to collect Marcus."

Dessie's heart sank. There would be no chance for any kind of romantic reunion with Rory for the moment. Their eyes met. Rory shrugged. "That's fine," Dessie said. "Thanks."

Jules looked up from making tea. "You can have your honeymoon when the snow melts. Just a few days, the met office said. You'll have to take cold showers until then, my friends. Or…you can go to Clodagh and ask if she'll give you a room."

"I'd rather cut my wrists and jump off a cliff," Rory muttered. "Okay, I'll take Dessie into town and collect Marcus. I have to go and see the solicitors anyway."

Jules smiled. "Good idea. Make yourself useful. I hope Clodagh won't make a fuss about selling the farm. But this weather should help make up her mind."

"If she does make a fuss, it could take months before we can sell," Rory said glumly. "Then I might lose the chance to buy that little stud farm in England."

Dessie jumped up. "Let's go there right now. You have to let her know what you're up to. You also have to confront her with the fact that if you and Orla want to sell, she has to agree. That's the law, isn't it?"

"It certainly is," Jules agreed.

Rory gathered up their jackets drying in front of the stove. "Okay. Let's go, then. Let's go and fight for our future."

Dessie buttoned her jacket with trembling fingers. If Clodagh was anything like her mother, there might be a long battle before she agreed. Not that she could refuse, but she could certainly stall long enough for Rory to lose out on the stud farm he had fallen in love with. He deserved it after all he'd been through. But would Clodagh understand that? Probably not. Dessie clenched her teeth. Rory might crumble under pressure, but not Dessie Broadbent. *Chutzpah*, she thought, *I'll show them what that means.*

CHAPTER 25

They found the house in darkness, except for a light in the window of the study beside the kitchen.

"Someone is there at least," Rory said as they got out of the jeep. "Let's go and have a look."

They shuffled carefully through the snow to the back door, which swung open when Rory pulled at it. He groped for the light switch. The kitchen light revealed a recently consumed meal of sausages and baked beans.

"Where is everybody?" Dessie asked, looking around. "It's freezing in here. The stove hasn't been lit, and the heating seems to be on the blink."

"The boiler must have seized up again," Rory remarked. "It's a bit of a bastard to get it going." He took Dessie's hand, and together they made their way down the corridor to the study. Rory opened the door.

Clodagh, sitting at the desk littered with papers, looked at them in surprise. "Jesus, you gave me a fright. What the hell are you doing here?"

"I have something to tell you," Rory said. "Not just me. Dessie and me, actually."

"Really?" Clodagh flicked through the papers. "Then you could start by telling me what the feck all this is. Bills and more bills. Cattle feed for several hundred euros. Don't cattle eat grass? Why do they need all this feed? And vet's bills, what's that all about? Plus, the rep says we have to pay a fine because the cattle have been grazing near the river, which harms the environment."

"Welcome to modern farming," Rory replied. "That's just a fraction of what we have to pay. I take it you haven't seen the water bill yet? A cow drinks about fifty litres a day, more in hot weather. We—I mean you—have a hundred and thirty head of cattle. You do the maths."

"But what about the income?" Clodagh asked. "Don't we make money here?"

Rory nodded and pulled out a folder from the shelf beside the desk. "It's all here. Income and outgoings. We're actually doing quite well this year. I sold a large number of bullocks only last month. We should be about even, with about three thousand in profit. Which, of course, will be divided between the three of us."

Clodagh glared at Rory. "So I get around a thousand a month? To feed and clothe a whole family?"

"Something like that," Rory said. "I supplement my income with my horse business, of course. But that has nothing to do with you."

Clodagh jumped up from her chair. "What do you mean? Those horses grazed here on our land. They were stabled in our stables. I'd say they're very much our horses, not yours."

"They're mine," Rory snapped. "I have papers to prove it. In any case, all this is immaterial. I don't know if you've spoken to Orla, but—"

Clodagh's eyes narrowed. "Yes, I have. I know you both want to sell. But I don't. Not yet anyway." She suddenly seemed to notice Dessie. "What's she doing here?"

Rory put his arm around Dessie. "She's here because we're going to get married."

Clodagh's jaw dropped. "What? You're going to marry that, that...slut?"

"Shut up, Clodagh," Rory snarled. "I won't have you insult Dessie like that."

Clodagh pointed a shaking finger at Dessie. "But that's exactly what she is. If you don't know why she left town in such a hurry all those years ago, I'll tell you. She only went and slept with her sister's husband. How's that for a nice Protestant girl, eh?"

"That's a pack of lies and you know it," Rory replied. "Nobody believes it anymore anyway."

"I heard she was quite, eh, *popular* at university. I think she must have slept with every guy in her year," Clodagh stated.

Dessie smirked. "Yeah, well you have to kiss a lot of frogs before you find your prince."

Rory let out a snort of laughter. "Who didn't sow a few wild oats in their youth? Can't say I was the good little choir-boy myself. So grow up, okay? Let's talk business. You know that you'll eventually have to either buy Orla and me out or agree to selling."

Clodagh smirked. "I might delay things a bit, though. Just for fun."

"While you sink further into debt?" Dessie enquired. She flicked her fingers at the pile of bills. "You'll look pretty stupid being sued for all these things. Rory has kept this farm going with profit all these years. But here you are, not able to pay even the water bill. They'll turn off the water, and you'll have a huge herd screaming with thirst. That's pretty cruel. What do you think the farmers around here will say about that?"

Clodagh looked away. "That's not going to happen. I'll pay the bills."

"Where's the rest of the family?" Rory asked. "I didn't see anyone when we arrived."

"They…" Clodagh stopped. "They went back to Dublin to stay with Pat's sister for a while. The kids were a bit… unsettled. It'll take them a while to get used to country living. It's quite different from being here in the summer for a short holiday."

"God, yes. The country dream kind of loses its gloss in the winter," Dessie said, trying to keep the laughter from her voice. She looked at Clodagh, taking in her pale face, clenched jaw, and the stressed-out look in her eyes. Here was a woman facing disaster but too stubborn and too mean to admit it. "Clodagh," she said, her voice softer. "Why don't you give in? Why don't you admit that you can't do it? Rory doesn't want to keep the farm. He wants to walk away from all the sad memories and the pain. He wants to start afresh, make a new life and finally be happy. Why don't you? This farm will fetch a cool seven million, maybe more."

Clodagh stared at her. "What? Is that true?"

Dessie nodded. "It certainly is. You could walk away with around two and half million euros. Enough to send your kids to great schools and universities. You could buy a fabulous house, your husband could start up a business, you could go shopping in New York, or scuba dive in the Bahamas, or—" she paused "—whatever you heart desires, instead of sitting here in a freezing cold house running a farm that pays peanuts. I know what I'd pick, and it's not getting chilblains and wrinkles from trying to eke out a living in the back of beyond." Exhausted after her long tirade, Dessie drew breath. "That is, of course, unless you're devoted to the land your ancestors fought for all those centuries ago."

Clodagh stared back at Dessie. She was quiet for a long time, during which Rory squeezed Dessie's hand so hard it hurt.

"Oookaayy," Clodagh finally said. "I think you made a point there. Screw the ancestors." She glanced at the bills on the desk then at Rory. "Mam wouldn't be happy. But she's dead, so what can she do? Seven million, huh? Why didn't you tell me?"

Rory shrugged. "I didn't think money was that important to you."

"That amount is pretty hard to walk away from." Clodagh

smiled. "The Bahamas? Shopping in New York? That beats getting up to look at cows every fecking morning." She got up and grabbed Rory's hand. "Let's do it! Let's sell this shite place and live a little!" She suddenly threw her arms around Dessie. "Thank you. Thank you so much for making me see that…well, money does make the world go around. My world, anyway."

Dessie hugged her back, the thought that Breda would be turning in her grave making her laugh out loud. *I won*, she thought, *I finally got my revenge.*

Rory put his arms around Clodagh. "Welcome back, sis. I don't know what made you turn into a clone of Mam, but I'm so happy to have the old Clodagh back."

Clodagh sniffed and wiped her eyes. "Don't know either. It was like Mam was haunting me. She wanted me to take over from her, I think. I went to see her a few months ago. She kept telling me not to let you take over the farm, that we women have to stick together. You know what she was like, so bloody *persuasive*."

"I know," Rory said. "But now we have to sort everything out before we put the place on the market. Not the best time to do it, but we'll have to get started. It's a great farm, the best land, and we'll sell it fully stocked. The house is big and needs a lick of paint here and there, but it's solid and the roof is good."

"Maybe we can smarten it up a bit?" Clodagh suggested. "Put in a new kitchen and bathroom. Pat's a builder. He'll do it all for free and get some of his lads to help. Shouldn't cost much to make it all look great."

"Some of the rooms are lovely," Dessie said. "I think this will sell very well once the house has been freshened up. After all, the economy is recovering. Farms like this are very much in demand."

"Will you stay here with me?" Clodagh asked. "I mean both of you? You can have the master bedroom. I didn't move in there yet, so it's still the same."

Rory glanced at Dessie. "Okay. We'll stay here. Dessie's stuff is in the jeep anyway."

Clodagh let out a deep sigh. "Fabulous. We can get started straight away. I'll just have to call Pat and tell him."

Rory pulled out a chair for Dessie. "Won't he be disappointed?"

"With the prospect of making two and a half million and not having to become a farmer?" Clodagh laughed. "He'll be over the moon. And the kids? They'll be ecstatic. They were never really into country life, to be honest."

Dessie sat down with Clodagh beside her, and Rory started to sift through the papers on the desk. Outside, the sun rose on snow-covered fields and shone on the old farm, where peace reigned at last.

EPILOGUE

Miranda's Christmas party turned into a crowded, noisy evening. Dessie, all dressed up in a green silk dress, felt like pinching herself. This had to be a dream. Here she was, engaged to Rory and staying at his farm while they all worked hard to do up the house prior to putting it on the market in early January. It was incredible to think that Rory had decided to not only leave his farm and his home town, but also to move to England to start his own stud farm, where they would live together as husband and wife. She glanced yet again at the emerald surrounded by tiny diamonds on her finger, trying to take it all in. It was true, it was happening and she was finally complete.

Dessie looked around the table, at the four boys at one end: Aidan, so grown-up, already at university; Jules' son, Tony, with his blue eyes and reddish-blonde hair so like Harry it made her heart ache; and the younger boys chatting and arguing and throwing bread rolls at each other. Then Jules and Marcus opposite her, deep in conversation, their body language an obvious clue to their relationship. Jules was in sparkling form, her eyes shining, her face glowing with happiness, smiling at Marcus, who returned her smile with such tenderness it made Dessie tear up. Jules happy at last. With the most unlikely man in the world.

"Gravy?" Jerry asked beside her, passing her the sauce boat.

"Oh, thank you." Dessie dribbled gravy on her turkey and roast potatoes. "Sorry. I was miles away. Just going through all the events since I came here."

"You certainly stirred things up," Jerry said, laughing. "Sorry I wasn't here much the past month. But I was busy up in Dublin and here too with Miranda's organic farm and some discussions with the bank. We'll have to take loan to buy those fields from Rory."

"I'm sorry if that causes problems."

"No, not really. We tried to buy them from Breda years ago, but she always refused. Now we have a chance to correct that. We're very happy. I hope the probate won't take too long."

Dessie passed the sauce boat to Rory. "No, the solicitor said it would come through in a couple of weeks. And we've also had offers from two farmers nearby who want to buy up the land for tillage. Much more lucrative than beef cattle. Then we'll hang on to twenty acres that will go with the sale of the house."

Jerry nodded. "Good idea. Tillage is the way to go around here. The soil is so fertile you could stick your finger in the ground at it'd sprout leaves. Our fruit and vegetable farm is doing well, and I think one of our boys will join us once he's out of school. He wants to study horticulture."

"And Aiden, your eldest? I hear he's thinking of going into politics?"

Jerry nodded. "Yes. There's no stopping him. But why not? If that's what he wants to do. I think he'll be good at it."

"I think he'll be brilliant," Dessie said. "I read all about the anti-bullying campaign and the website he started with Finola. Amazing work by the two of them."

Finola, on Jerry's other side, leaned forward. "It was all Aiden. I was just helping him along. He's the true star. Love your dress, by the way. What do you call that pale green?"

"Eau de Nil," Dessie said, admiring Finola's red silk shirt.

"I might return the compliment. That shirt is exquisite. And wearing it with skinny jeans is so cool. Not something I'd pull off. But then, I'm sure you were born cool. I bet your parents said 'What a cool baby' when you were born."

Finola laughed. "Nah, I think my dad said 'Shite, it's a girl.' He wanted another boy. So I tried my best to become one. Nearly succeeded until I met Colin. He turned me back into a girl. Didn't you, sweetie?" she shouted across the table at her husband, who was deep in conversation with Audrey.

Colin looked up. "Did what, baby?"

"Turn me into a girl," Finola repeated.

Colin laughed. "I didn't turn you into anything, hon. I love you the way you are. Strong, stroppy, and impossible to tame." He blew her a kiss and turned back to Audrey.

"Audrey looks positively dangerous tonight," Jerry declared. "Are you sure it was a good idea to put Colin beside her?"

Finola shrugged. "Ah, sure, isn't he always surrounded by gorgeous actresses? If he were going to stray, he'd do it with one of them. But you know what? I trust him. Crazy, huh?"

"Insane," Dessie agreed, knowing she'd be mad with jealousy if Rory paid that much attention to another woman, especially one as gorgeous as Audrey.

"Yeah, well," Finola said. "We have this pact. No fooling around in secret. If one of us is suddenly so attracted to someone else that we want to have an affair, we'll just say it and split up. There'll be no inbetween or quick flings or anything. It's either/or. So far neither of us have felt the urge. Don't think we will to be honest. It took us long enough to find each other. We've both been around the block so many times. And now that we have the girls, we're a family. That's something neither of us want to lose. Except—" she paused. "—the nitty-gritty of changing babies is not his thing. Nor mine, but I didn't wimp out, like a certain Hollywood star, who always has something better to do when they poop.

But hey, so what? It's not like they're going to be in nappies forever."

"Wise words," Jerry said. "You're becoming sensible at last."

Finola blew on a lock of hair. "Sensible, moi? Nah, that'll never happen." She grabbed her glass. "Hey, now that the dinner's nearly over and all we have to do is set fire to the pudding and hope the curtains won't go as well, I'd like to propose a toast."

"Good idea," Jerry said and raised his glass. "What shall we toast to?"

"First of all, Miranda and her scrumptious dinner," Dessie cut in, holding her glass high. "Miranda, you did it again!"

Miranda, on the other side of Colin, laughed and lifted her glass. "Thank you. And I want to drink to the happy couple."

"Which one?" Finola shouted as Marcus and Jules stole a quick kiss. "Everyone seems to be in love tonight."

"Not me," said Audrey, laughing, "even though I got to sit beside the heartthrob of the century. But he's immune to my charms." She pulled a mock sad face.

Colin winked at her. "I wouldn't say that. I fully appreciate your assets, darlin'. But I'm only allowed to window-shop these days."

"Well, that's a relief," Audrey sighed. "But to be honest, romance isn't number one on my agenda right now. I need to find permanent accommodation. And my bosses have announced a new look and layout for The Knockmealdown News. We need to move with the times, it appears. So, I'm going to be busy."

"You're welcome to stay here as long as you want," Miranda said. "The boys adore you. And I truly appreciate the help with their homework."

"Cheers!" Rory called. "Can we drink now? To love and to all the beautiful women here tonight." He knocked back his wine to communal laughter.

"To Audrey," Jerry called raising his glass again. "What a trooper!"

Then they cleared the plates, Miranda brought in the pudding doused in brandy, and Jerry put a match to it.

Dessie held Rory's hand while she watched the flames licking the twig of holly at the top of the pudding. "Just like the old days. Sitting here, at this old table, brings me back to when I was about eight and so excited about Christmas. My parents and my granny were still alive, and my big sisters were my heroes. Well, in a way, they still are."

Rory put his arm around her waist. "I prefer the new days. The past is the past. Let's look forward. So much to do before we can settle down. Lots of hard work. Are you ready?"

"More than ready, sweetheart."

"Do you think we should tell them?"

"Of course. But I think everyone knows already."

"I want to make it official." He cleared his throat and knocked his spoon against his glass. "While the pudding is being served, I have an announcement. Dessie and I have just become engaged, as you all know. And we're going to get married here in Cloughmichael at the end of January. Then we're moving to England as soon as all the details have been worked out and we've signed the contract for the stud farm we're buying."

"I think we knew most of that already," Miranda said as she handed out pudding around the table. "But not that the wedding was going to be so soon."

"And there's something else," Dessie cut in. "We're going to have an addition to the family."

There was a brief silence. "What?" Jules shouted. "You're having a baby?"

Miranda hugged Dessie. "That's wonderful. I'm so happy for you. Where will it be born? In England?"

"No," Rory said, "in the barn at the old farm." He continued after the laughter died down. "We don't want to move her until after the birth."

"That's right," Dessie agreed. "We don't know how many there'll be yet."

"There's more than one?" Audrey asked.

"Three, we think," Dessie replied.

"Three?" Jules squealed, looking at Dessie's slim waist. "Are you sure?"

"Yes," Rory replied. "But Fergal said—"

"Fergal? The vet?" Finola roared with laughter. "Holy shit, it's the dog! Nellie's having puppies. Am I right?"

Dessie winked. "Yes. I was wondering how long we could keep you going."

Jules threw her napkin at Rory. "Very funny."

"Well, I thought it was a bit cruel to have Dessie give birth in the barn," Jerry added.

"So there you go," Finola sighed. "A happy ending, a new arrival, love all around. The prodigal daughter came back and all was forgiven. I couldn't have written a better story myself."

THE END

About the author

Susanne O'Leary is the bestselling author of more than twenty novels, mainly in the romantic fiction genre. She has also written three crime novels and two in the historical fiction genre. She has been the wife of a diplomat (still is), a fitness teacher and a translator. She now writes full-time from either of two locations; a rambling house in County Tipperary, Ireland or a little cottage overlooking the Atlantic in Dingle, County Kerry. When she is not scaling the mountains of said counties, keeping fit in the local gym, or doing yoga, she keeps writing, producing a book every six months.

Find out more about Susanne and her books on her website: http://www.susanne-oleary.co.uk

Printed in Great Britain
by Amazon